Dawn Keeler

DAISY MILLER

Adapted in collaboration with Adolf Wood
from the story by Henry James

T0348083

OBERON BOOKS
LONDON

WWW.OBERONBOOKS.COM

First published in this adaptation in 2005 by Oberon Books Ltd.
521 Caledonian Road, London N7 9RH
Tel: +44 (0) 20 7607 3637 / Fax: +44 (0) 20 7607 3629
e-mail: info@oberonbooks.com
www.oberonbooks.com

A catalogue record for this book is available from the British Library.

Cover illustration: Andrzej Klimowski

ISBN: 978-1-84002-598-9

Contents

Foreword

by John Fraser

ON A SUMMER'S DAY in 1999, Dawn Keeler arrived at my farmhouse in Italy with a package under her arm. Several masterpieces were hatching in my brain, and she knew that I would be reluctant to abandon my Tuscan retreat while they remained unwritten, but she had a proposition to make, and she refused to leave till I had read the contents of the envelope. Inside were two one-act plays, *Roman Fever*, based on a short story by Edith Wharton, and *Daisy Miller*, adapted from the novella of the same name by Henry James: Dawn saw these two stories as naturally linked together, not only by their common theme of death by 'Roman fever', but also by the close friendship and mutual admiration of their authors. She wanted me to direct a rehearsed reading of the plays as a double bill, and in anticipation of my acceptance she had already booked the Actors Centre in London for an evening in November.

I was immediately persuaded by the subject-matter and the quality of the writing that this would be an exciting project. There was no money for fees, so assembling an able cast might prove a stumbling block.

As it turned out, for that reading in November 1999, we had a cast made in heaven. Emilia Fox was Daisy, Ben Miles, Winterbourne. The women in the two plays were Lucinda Curtis and Valerie Sarruf.

The evening was such a success, that Dawn was encouraged to amplify *Daisy Miller*, and this is the result: an original play – based on Henry James – a play which retells the moving story of a young woman from the New World out of her depth in the treacherous currents of Old Europe; it also captures for the audience the Jamesian virtues, implicit rather than explicit, of reference rather than exposition, of peripheral vision rather than direct appraisal. It has all the pitilessly honest observation of The Master, and it pays an affectionate tribute to the beguiling and contradictory foibles of humanity. Never passing judgement, some might even say rarely coming to conclusions, it is Henry James's style to leave the reader to decide.

True to James's spirit, Dawn Keeler respects the intelligence of her audience.

She has written a play that you will be talking about long after you have seen – or read – it.

John Fraser, 2005

Preface
by Adolf Wood

Scandal and Success: How *Daisy Miller* Brought Fame to Henry James

DAISY MILLER, Henry James's classic novella, aptly described by one critic as a 'dark comedy of manners', was first published in 1878. After the initial *succès de scandale* provoked by its depiction of fatally misunderstood innocence, with high society matrons in America voicing their outrage at what they saw as a horrible caricature of the 'American Girl' misbehaving in Europe, and others just as passionately defending her character, publication of *Daisy Miller* brought its young American author international celebrity. Henry James was then only 35; and although in his immensely productive later years he came to be regarded by his peers in the literary world with respect and admiration, amounting to reverence – they dubbed him 'The Master' – in his own lifetime he never regained the wide popularity that *Daisy Miller* had earned him.

No major novelist was more uncompromisingly, more heroically, dedicated to his art than James. At the same time, he craved recognition from the public at large, and was saddened by what he saw as its unfair neglect of his works. At various times he tried his hand at writing plays for the commercial theatre, hoping to emulate the success of his fashionable contemporary, Oscar Wilde; but his efforts ended in failure and ignominy (including boos and catcalls at the first night of his play *Guy Domville*). He wrote a preposterously bad adaptation for the stage of *Daisy Miller*, giving it a woefully incongruous happy ending and stiff doses of melodramatic nonsense. Mercifully, it never saw the light of theatrical day, being rejected in New York and London, and James was spared even further humiliation. It is a large and poignant irony that the novels and tales of James the failed dramatist have, in the modern era, yielded such a vast

number of successful dramatisations for the stage and screen
– *Washington Square* (*The Heiress*), *The Aspern Papers*, *The Turn of the Screw, The Portrait of a Lady*, to name but a few.

Whatever the ups and downs of Henry James's reputation – and since at least the mid-twentieth century it has been enormously on the 'up' (witness, for example, the flurry of recently published novels by Cólm Toíbin, David Lodge and others, consciously celebrating their authors' indebtedness to 'The Master') – the character of Daisy herself seems to enjoy a perennial freshness, despite, or perhaps partly because of, the sad fate that befalls her. In accounting for the enduring popularity of her story, the American critic Edmund Wilson saw it as 'certainly due to her creator's having somehow conveyed the impression that her spirit went marching on'.

Adolf Wood, 2005

Synopsis

A BUSTLING HOLIDAY RESORT on the shore of Lake Geneva in Switzerland, summer, 1878. Daisy Miller, a charming, beautiful, but uncultivated American girl who is 'doing' Europe with her mother and younger brother, meets Frederick Winterbourne, an American expatriate, in the garden of the palatial hotel where he is staying with his aunt, Mrs Costello, a wealthy and ferociously snobbish New York socialite. Winterbourne, a writer of travel articles for an American newspaper, is immediately captivated by Daisy, who delights in her power over him and teases him for being too 'stiff'. From the very beginning of their relationship, as he later confides to his diary, he is assailed by inner doubts about Daisy's character and intentions. Is she merely a typical young American flirt? Is she really as innocent as she seems? Or is there a darker, perhaps unscrupulous side to her nature? Having lived in Europe for so many years, he fears he is dangerously out of touch with the ways of the new generation in America. On their side, the nouveau-riche Millers have no perception of the complex code that underlies behaviour in European society, and Winterbourne is astonished at the girl's feisty independence, and her mother's naïve unconcern when Daisy accompanies him alone on a delightfully flirtatious trip to the nearby Château de Chillon. He defends her, however, to Mrs Costello, who denounces the Millers as 'common'.

Rome is the next stage of the Millers' tour; Winterbourne by coincidence will also be in the city when they make their visit, and he looks forward with pleasurable anticipation to seeing Daisy again. He meets the Millers at a soirée given by his friend Mrs Walker, a widow and fellow American expatriate. Winterbourne learns with dismay that Daisy has scandalised the American colony in Rome by being seen constantly with Giovanelli, an obscure Italian lawyer, suspected of being a fortune hunter. Mrs Costello, with whom Winterbourne is staying in her Rome apartment, angrily tries to persuade Winterbourne not to see Daisy any more, as does Mrs Walker, who had at first taken Daisy under her wing, but now thinks her 'intrigue' has gone too far. Winterbourne declines to take their advice and seeks out Daisy, warning her that she is in danger of being ostracised by the American community in Rome if she continues to see Giovanelli. A few days later, against all advice, Daisy goes to the Colosseum with Giovanelli after dark, contracts 'Roman fever' (malaria), and dies. At her funeral Giovanelli tells Winterbourne that Daisy was 'the most beautiful young lady I ever saw, and the most amiable. Also – the most innocent.' Winterbourne finds some consolation in Mrs Miller's disclosure that before her death Daisy's thoughts were for him.

To Milly

Acknowledgements

I WANT TO THANK, above all, my husband, Adolf Wood, for his invaluable help, advice, and belief in this play. My agent, Gordon Dickerson, for his unwavering faith, tenacity, and honest opinions. John Fraser, for directing a rehearsed reading of *Daisy* in the early stages, and for his encouragement ever since. Keith Baxter, for his support, and conviction that *Daisy* would eventually be produced. Monty Haltrecht and Nicky Amer, for their constant kindness and support. Lucinda Curtis and Faith Brook, for their beautiful performances in a rehearsed reading. They have all helped me to keep writing, and to keep believing in, this touching story.

My thanks also to Ian Fricker for taking the plunge and producing the play, Christopher Morahan, for directing it, with such care and thoughtfulness, Christopher Woods for his beautiful design, and all the other members of the production team. Last, but not least, my thanks to the cast who have brought *Daisy Miller* to life.

Dawn Keeler, 2005

Characters

DAISY MILLER
Young American

FREDERICK WINTERBOURNE
Young American living in Europe

MRS MILLER
Daisy's mother

MRS COSTELLO
Winterbourne's aunt

MRS WALKER
American widow

GIOVANELLI
Italian lawyer

EUGENIO
Swiss courier

WAITER

SERVANT

The play takes place in 1878–9, in Vevey, a resort on Lake Geneva, Switzerland, and Rome, Italy.

Daisy Miller was first performed at the Malvern Festival Theatre on 30 August 2005, with the following cast:

FREDERICK WINTERBOURNE, Richard Grieve

DAISY MILLER, Scarlett Johnson

MRS COSTELLO, Jean Boht

MRS MILLER, Sandra Dickinson

MRS WALKER, Shirley Anne Field

EUGENIO/GIOVANELLI, Craig Giovanelli

Producer, Ian Fricker

Director, Christopher Morahan

Designer, Christopher Woods

Lighting Designer, Gerry Jenkinson

Music, Ilona Sekacz

ACT ONE

FREDERICK WINTERBOURNE is sitting, smoking, at a table.
He is engrossed in writing. The sound of a pen scratching on paper.
A cup of coffee is on the table. The stage is dark apart from a light
on WINTERBOURNE.

WINTERBOURNE: (*Voice over.*) July the sixteenth, 1879,
  the Hôtel des Trois Couronnes, Vevey. Here I am back
  in Switzerland, at the little resort of Vevey, just two
  months after that whole remarkable and mystifying
  episode came to an end. It was in this very garden,
  almost a year ago, that I first met Daisy Miller: real
  name Annie, Annie P Miller from Schenectady, in
  the State of New York…the incomparable Daisy! If I
  wrote here all that I could write about what happened
  in the days, weeks and months after that meeting, I
  should speedily fill this notebook, bought in Rome last
  winter, but hitherto unopened. It's so long since I've
  kept any notes, written down my current reflections,
  taken a sheet of paper, as it were, into my confidence.
  (*WINTERBOURNE starts to speak in sync with his voice*
  and gradually takes over.) Perhaps it is too late now fully to
  recapture that experience, but I want to catch and keep
  its essence, distil its meaning. Whether I succeed, or not,
  I'm glad I've come back here, where it all started – it is
  something that I have had to do. (*WINTERBOURNE*
  has put down his pen and addresses the audience.) Vevey
  in June is always the same; American travellers are
  so numerous at this time that it takes on some of the
  qualities of an American watering-place. There's a
  flitting to and fro of stylish young girls, a rustling of
  muslin flounces. One of those young girls last June,
  surely the most striking of all, was Miss Daisy Miller.

Gradually, a light comes up on DAISY. She is standing as though in a painting. Quite still. The arbour acts as a frame for the painting.

WINTERBOURNE continues.

What am I supposed to do? Ignore her? I watch her, fascinated. Everything about her, her eyes, her nose, her ears, her teeth, her complexion, all are perfection. I immediately want to talk to her. But I hesitate. In Geneva, the dark little capital of Calvinism, where I've mainly lived since a boy, a young man isn't at liberty to speak to a young unmarried girl, except under quite exceptional circumstances! *Quel absurdité!* But here, in pleasure-loving Vevey, with so many American tourists milling around, it seems the most natural thing in the world.

Lights up. Vevey, on Lake Geneva, Switzerland, June 1878. The garden of the Hôtel des Trois Couronnes.

Sound of a brass band playing a Strauss waltz floats across the lake.

DAISY MILLER steps out of the picture. She goes and stands in front of WINTERBOURNE. She carries a parasol and has a small pair of binoculars on a ribbon round her neck.

That music is very jolly, isn't it?

DAISY: It makes one want to dance.

She moves a little in time to the music.

WINTERBOURNE: Presumably that's what it's meant to do. Do you know the music?

DAISY: No.

WINTERBOURNE: It's a waltz.

DAISY: I know it's a waltz, I thought you meant that particular waltz. Everyone's waltzing in New York these days. (*She leans over the table.*) What are you writing?

WINTERBOURNE: A set of articles for a New York newspaper, about places in Europe I've enjoyed visiting. I'm hoping they will be published as a travel book.

DAISY: A guidebook!

WINTERBOURNE: Well, yes, it will contain some useful information about places, but it won't exactly be a Baedeker!

DAISY: A Baedeker? What's that?

WINTERBOURNE: It's *the* guidebook – a bible for the discriminating traveller!

DAISY: Dear me!

WINTERBOURNE: (*After a silence.*) Isn't this a simply tremendous view? See that mountain over there?

DAISY: It's so big, I couldn't miss it, I guess! But I don't know what it's called. Our Swiss courier, Eugenio, has been too busy chasing after my brother Randolph to tell us much about the area.

WINTERBOURNE: Oh, your brother and I have already made acquaintance. He told me his name. We had quite a conversation. He's a most spirited little boy.

DAISY: Randolph spirited? I'll say! And so naughty. He was jumping round on a pole just now, pretending it was a horse. Not only that, he was poking it into everything he could find. I thought he was going to poke my eyes out.

WINTERBOURNE: That would have been a pity. You have, if I may say so, rather remarkable eyes.

DAISY looks at him quizzically.

By the way, the pole's an alpenstock.

DAISY: I know, it's just easier to call it a pole.

WINTERBOURNE: Randolph told me he's going to climb the Alps with it... Are you going to Italy?

DAISY: Yes, sir. I'm going to Rome for the winter – with my mother and Randolph – and of course Eugenio.

WINTERBOURNE: Are you thinking of going over the Simplon?

DAISY: Going over the what?

WINTERBOURNE: The Simplon.

DAISY: I don't know. I suppose it's some mountain.

WINTERBOURNE: Yes, it is. *Some* mountain! The scenery is quite spectacular. From Vevey, crossing the Simplon Pass is the best way of going down into Italy.

DAISY: (*Looking through her binoculars.*) What's that mountain over there?

WINTERBOURNE: It's the *Dent du Midi. Dent* is French for 'tooth'; *du Midi* means 'of the South'.

DAISY: 'Tooth of the South'! I suppose it does look like a tooth, an upside down one. Do you live up in the mountains?

WINTERBOURNE: (*Laughing.*) Good gracious, I'm not a goatherd! No, I live in Geneva, just across the lake.

DAISY: Have you lived there very long?

WINTERBOURNE: Yes, indeed. I've travelled a good deal too. I'm very fond of travelling, and happily, as a writer for an American newspaper, I've been able to do it.

DAISY: I suppose you know ever so many foreign languages?

WINTERBOURNE: Yes, quite a few.

DAISY: Is it hard to learn to speak them?

WINTERBOURNE: Yes, to speak them well it is. Have you picked up any foreign words on your tour?

DAISY: Just the odd one. But I don't want to speak foreign languages; I just want to listen to them. They say the way they speak in the French theatre is so beautiful.

WINTERBOURNE: Absolutely true.

DAISY: Have you been to the French theatre very often?

WINTERBOURNE: The first time I was in Paris I went every night.

DAISY: Goodness, every night! And when we were in Paris I didn't go once.

WINTERBOURNE: Why not?

DAISY: Randolph, of course. He doesn't want to go anywhere. He'd like to be back at home with Father. (*Pause.*) Do you have a favourite country in Europe?

WINTERBOURNE: Yes. There's one I love beyond any other.

DAISY: Which is that?

WINTERBOURNE: Italy. It's a beautiful place.

DAISY: Well, I'll get a chance to see it, won't I? (*Pointing with her parasol.*) Have you been to that old castle?

WINTERBOURNE: The Château de Chillon. More than once.

DAISY: We haven't been there. I *want* to go there, dreadfully. I mean to go there. I wouldn't go away from here without seeing that old castle.

WINTERBOURNE: It's a very pretty excursion, and very easy to make. You can go in a carriage, you know, or by the little steamer.

DAISY: You can go in the little train.

WINTERBOURNE: Yes, you can.

DAISY: Our courier says they take you right up to the castle. We were going last week, but Mother gave out. She suffers dreadfully from dyspepsia. She said she couldn't go... Randolph wouldn't go either. But I guess we'll go this week if we can get him to go.

WINTERBOURNE: Your brother isn't interested in ancient monuments?

DAISY: No, he says he doesn't care much about old castles. He's only nine. He wants to stay at the hotel. Mother's afraid to leave him alone, and Eugenio won't stay with him; so we haven't been to many places. But it will be too bad if we don't go up there.

WINTERBOURNE: I should think it might be arranged. Couldn't you get someone to stay – for the afternoon – with Randolph?

DAISY: I wish *you'd* stay with him.

WINTERBOURNE: I'd much rather go to Chillon with you.

DAISY: With me?

WINTERBOURNE: *And* with your mother!

DAISY: I guess Mother won't go after all. She don't like to ride round in the afternoon. But did you really mean you'd like to go up there?

WINTERBOURNE: Certainly.

DAISY: Then we may arrange it. If Mother will stay with Randolph, I guess Eugenio will too; he doesn't like to stay with Randolph; he's the most fastidious man I ever saw. But he's a splendid courier, so I guess he'll stay at home with Randolph if mother does, and then *we* can go to the castle.

WINTERBOURNE: We?

DAISY: Yes, we! But Eugenio won't like me going with you. He wants to show it to us himself.

WINTERBOURNE: I'm sure we can overcome his objections.

DAISY: Eugenio likes to be in on everything we do. He seems to have taken over mother completely; but I guess she likes it. She can't really manage Randolph on her own. She misses my father, you see. My father and Randolph get on just fine.

WINTERBOURNE: I suppose Randolph could be a bit of a handful.

DAISY: He's bored. He doesn't like travelling. He's got nobody to play with. He needs a teacher. Mother is looking for a tutor for him. An English lady we met on the train – I think her name was Miss Featherstone; perhaps you know her. She wanted to know why I didn't give Randolph lessons – give him *instruction* she called it. I guess he could give me more instruction than I could give him. He's very smart.

WINTERBOURNE: Yes, he seems very smart.

DAISY: Can you get good teachers in Italy?

WINTERBOURNE: Very good, I should think.

DAISY: Miss Featherstone asked me if we didn't all live in hotels in America. I told her I had never been in so many hotels in my life as since I came to Europe. It's nothing but hotels.

WINTERBOURNE: Randolph told me he wants to go back to America because the candy is better there!

DAISY: I know. He's convinced that American candy is the best in the world. Well, he'll have to wait. We are going to Rome for the winter whatever happens. (*Still looking through the binoculars.*) What's that hotel over there with hundreds of balconies?

WINTERBOURNE: And with all the flags flying?

DAISY: Yes!

WINTERBOURNE: It's the Grand Hotel.

DAISY: It reminds me of Congress Hall in Saratoga Springs. My father took us there last year. It has one thousand rooms. Have you been to Saratoga Springs?

WINTERBOURNE: No, I haven't, but I've stayed at the Ocean House in Newport, and this place often reminds me of Newport... How do you like Europe?

DAISY: Very much. It's perfectly sweet. I'm not disappointed, not one bit. The only thing I don't like is the society. There ain't *any* society – or if there is I don't know where it keeps itself. Do you? (*He looks baffled.*) You're the first gentleman I've met in Europe that has been at all attentive – or at all interesting, come to that!

WINTERBOURNE: I'm flattered.

DAISY: Maybe it's because you're American. You *are* American, aren't you?

WINTERBOURNE: Through and through, though I've lived in Europe a long time.

DAISY: At first I took you for a German, especially when you spoke.

WINTERBOURNE: I've met Germans who spoke like Americans, but never the other way round. I will have to brush up my accent.

DAISY: Oh, don't do that. I like the way you speak. It's much nicer than the New York accent. I come from Schenectady – if you know where that is.

WINTERBOURNE: Randolph told me you were from Schenectady. He also said your father owns a large business and is very rich.

DAISY: What else did he tell you?

WINTERBOURNE: That though you are called Daisy, your real name is Annie P Miller.

DAISY: Did he also tell you that I am very fond of society?

WINTERBOURNE: No, he didn't mention that.

DAISY: Well, I am. I'm *very* fond of it, and I've always had plenty of it. I don't mean only in Schenectady, but in New York City.

WINTERBOURNE: Won't you sit down, and you can tell me about it.

DAISY: I rather like hanging around. (*She looks him squarely in the face.*) Perhaps I will sit down after all. You can smoke if you like. I saw you smoking when I came into the garden. Eugenio smokes all the time... Last winter I had seventeen dinners given for me in New York, and three of them were by gentlemen. I have always had a great deal of gentlemen's society.

WINTERBOURNE: You must have many friends in New York.

DAISY: Oh, I do, more than in Schenectady – more gentlemen friends; and more young lady friends too.

WINTERBOURNE: My dear Miss Miller, I can promise you that when you're in Rome you'll have plenty of society.

DAISY: Do you know Rome well, then?

WINTERBOURNE: Yes, very well. I've been visiting it regularly for years. My aunt takes an apartment near the Spanish Steps. There are lots of Americans living in Rome – quite a colony in fact. I can introduce you to some of them, if you like.

DAISY: Tell me *all* about Rome.

WINTERBOURNE: To tell you all about Rome, I would need several weeks, if not months... Rome's even greater than its reputation. The first time I was there I went reeling through the streets in a fever of excitement, and it *still* has the power to excite me.

DAISY: More than anything?

WINTERBOURNE: (*Looks at her.*) Almost...anything.

DAISY: It seems you like Rome all right!

WINTERBOURNE: Nothing on earth can be compared to it.

DAISY: Why is it so special?

WINTERBOURNE: A thousand reasons. Take the Spanish Steps in the Piazza di Spagna, for example. When you stand in the Piazza early in the morning, with the sun coming up, with few people around, you are astonished by the variety of colours. The buildings are all different shades of pink, red, yellow, and in the morning sun they have a special glow about them.

DAISY: Go on.

WINTERBOURNE: At every corner you turn, there is something wondrous to behold: imposing churches, magnificent palaces, ancient ruins, beautiful gardens, triumphal arches, gigantic columns, fountains, pine trees...

DAISY: Go on, go on!

WINTERBOURNE: From the top of the Spanish Steps a road leads to the Pincio, on the edge of the Borghese Gardens, where the Villa Medici stands. You get a breathtaking view of the whole of Rome – of St Peter's, the biggest church in Christendom, of the Pantheon, and the Forum, where Caesar addressed the Romans, and the Colosseum, perhaps the world's most famous building, where Christian martyrs died and gladiators fought, and the Piazza di Spagna...

DAISY: Stop, stop! You're making me dizzy! Why are they called the Spanish Steps?

WINTERBOURNE: They were so named in the seventeenth century after the Spanish Embassy which occupied the palazzo in the square. One of the reasons it's so well known to English-speaking visitors is the fact that the poet John Keats died in a rooming house there in 1821.

DAISY: John Keats?

WINTERBOURNE: Yes, he who wrote the famous lines:

Beauty is truth, truth beauty – that is all
Ye know on earth, and all ye need to know.

DAISY: Do you believe that?

WINTERBOURNE: I'm not sure it's *all* you need to know, but it's a good place to start. The little house halfway up the steps on the right is where Keats rented a room. Shelley, Byron and many other poets, writers and musicians lived in the area.

DAISY: I've just had a perfectly splendid idea. You know I told you mother is looking for a teacher for Randolph, to travel around with us. Well, why don't you come as his tutor, you know so much about everything?

WINTERBOURNE: It's a very charming idea, but I have things to do in Geneva.

DAISY: What things?

WINTERBOURNE: Well, things!

A tall, handsome man with superb whiskers, wearing a velvet morning-coat and a brilliant watch-chain, approaches DAISY.

DAISY: Oh, Eugenio!

EUGENIO: (*Bowing to DAISY, after eyeing WINTERBOURNE from head to toe.*) Mademoiselle, I have been looking for an hour for Master Randolph. He's always here when he's not wanted and never when he is.

DAISY: I guess he's talking to that waiter.

EUGENIO: That waiter gives him sweets. He shouldn't talk to waiters.

Luncheon gong sounds.

I do what I can, Mademoiselle. I'm a courier, not a nurse. Mademoiselle, luncheon is waiting, and Madame is at the table.

DAISY: Tell mother to begin – I'm talking to a gentleman.

WINTERBOURNE: I should be very sorry to inconvenience your mother.

DAISY: See here, Eugenio. I'm going to that old castle, anyway.

EUGENIO: (*Put out.*) Mademoiselle has made arrangements?

DAISY: (*To WINTERBOURNE.*) You won't back out?

WINTERBOURNE: I shall not be happy till we go!

DAISY: And you're staying in this hotel?

WINTERBOURNE: Yes.

DAISY: And you're really American?

WINTERBOURNE: I shall have the honour of presenting you to a lady staying here, who'll tell you all about me.

DAISY: (*Flatly, almost dismissively.*) Oh well, we'll go some day. Come along, Eugenio. We'd better join mother for lunch.

She leaves without a backward glance, followed by EUGENIO.

WINTERBOURNE turns to the audience.

WINTERBOURNE: 'I've always had a great deal of gentlemen's society.' I am amused, but also baffled, by Daisy's remark. What does she mean? They could have been the words of a middle-aged *fille de joie*! I've never heard a young girl express herself in this way. I feel as if I've lived in Geneva so long that I've become morally muddled. I seem to have lost the right sense for the young American tone. Is she simply a pretty girl from New York State – are they all like that, the pretty girls who've had a good deal of gentlemen's society? Or is she a designing, an audacious, in short, an expert young person? Daisy *looks* extremely innocent. Some people have told me that American girls *are* exceedingly innocent...and others have told me that they are not.

How confusing! Certainly Daisy is very charming, and wonderfully communicative and easy! She is also very unsophisticated. I must take her for a harmless flirt – a pretty American flirt. She isn't the sort of dangerous coquette I've encountered before in Europe, women who are older than Daisy and provided, for respectability's sake, with husbands. I am grateful to have found a formula that applies to her. I shall now expose Daisy to my aunt's scrutiny – for better or for worse. (*He closes his notebook, drains the last of his coffee and puts the notebook back in his pocket.*) Alice Costello is my father's eldest sister. Widow of fortune from New York, a person of much distinction (in her own eyes), who considers herself very exclusive. In truth, a prodigious snob.

MRS COSTELLO enters.

Dear aunt, I hope your headache's better. I've been sitting in the garden waiting for you to recover.

MRS COSTELLO: I am quite well, now, Frederick. You know, if it hadn't been for my wretched headaches, I would have left my mark on the world.

WINTERBOURNE: I have no doubt you would have, aunt. (*Pause.*) I was wondering if you have noticed an American family staying in the hotel. A mamma, a daughter, and a little boy.

MRS COSTELLO: And a courier? Yes, I have noticed them. Seen them – heard them – and kept out of their way.

WINTERBOURNE: You don't approve of them.

MRS COSTELLO: They are very common, Frederick. They are the sort of Americans that one does one's duty by not accepting.

WINTERBOURNE: Ah, you don't accept them?

MRS COSTELLO: I can't my dear Frederick. I would if I could, but I can't.

WINTERBOURNE: The young girl *is* very pretty.

MRS COSTELLO: Of course she's pretty, but she is very common.

WINTERBOURNE: (*Pause.*) I see what you mean, of course.

MRS COSTELLO: She has that charming look they all have. I can't think where they pick it up; and she dresses to perfection –

WINTERBOURNE makes as if to agree with her but MRS COSTELLO cuts him off.

– no, you don't know how well she dresses. I can't think where they get their taste.

WINTERBOURNE: But, my dear aunt, Miss Daisy Miller is not a Comanche savage!

MRS COSTELLO: No, indeed, Comanche savages have more dignity. Be warned: she is a young lady who has an intimacy with her mamma's courier.

WINTERBOURNE: An intimacy with the courier?

MRS COSTELLO: Yes – there's no other name for such a relationship. Her silly little mother is just as bad! They treat the courier as a familiar friend – as a gentleman or a scholar. I shouldn't wonder if he dines with them. Very likely they have never seen a man with such good manners, such fine clothes, so *like* a gentleman. He probably corresponds to the young lady's idea of a Count. He sits with them in the garden, in the evening. I think he smokes.

WINTERBOURNE: Well, I am not a courier, and yet she was very charming to me.

MRS COSTELLO: You had better have said at first, that you had already made her acquaintance.

WINTERBOURNE: We simply met in the garden, and talked a bit.

MRS COSTELLO: *Tout bonnement!* And pray what did you say?

WINTERBOURNE: I said I should take the liberty of introducing her to my admirable aunt.

MRS COSTELLO: Your admirable aunt's a thousand times obliged to you.

WINTERBOURNE: It was to guarantee my respectability.

MRS COSTELLO: And pray who is to guarantee hers?

WINTERBOURNE: You are cruel! She's a very innocent girl.

MRS COSTELLO: You don't say that as if you believed it. You would never know her in America.

WINTERBOURNE: That seems a good reason for seizing the opportunity here. She *is* somewhat uncultivated, I grant you, but keen to learn. She is very nice and I am going to take her to the Château de Chillon.

MRS COSTELLO: You two are going off there together?

WINTERBOURNE: Yes.

MRS COSTELLO: Alone?

WINTERBOURNE: Yes.

MRS COSTELLO: She's very nice, you say? I should say it proved just the contrary. How long had you known her, may I ask, when this interesting project was devised? You haven't been in Vevey more than twenty-four hours.

WINTERBOURNE: I had known her half an hour!

MRS COSTELLO: Dear me! What a dreadful girl!

WINTERBOURNE: You really think that –

MRS COSTELLO: Think what, sir?

WINTERBOURNE: That she's the sort of young lady who expects a man – sooner or later – to carry her off?

MRS COSTELLO: I haven't the least idea what such young ladies expect a man to do. But I really think you had better not meddle with little American girls who are uncultivated, as you mildly put it. You would never have mixed with the likes of her in New York.

WINTERBOURNE: Aunt, that may be true, but I am not in New York.

MRS COSTELLO: I fear you've lived too long out of America. You'll be sure to make some great mistake. You're too innocent.

WINTERBOURNE: My dear aunt, I am not *so* innocent. Won't you let me introduce her to you then?

MRS COSTELLO: Is it literally true that she is going to the Château de Chillon with you?

WINTERBOURNE: I think she fully intends to, yes.

MRS COSTELLO: Then, my dear Frederick, I must decline the honour of her acquaintance. I am an old woman, but I am not too old – thank Heaven – to be shocked!

WINTERBOURNE: But don't they all perhaps do these things – the little American girls at home?

MRS COSTELLO: I should like to see my granddaughters do them!

WINTERBOURNE: From what I've heard, they are tremendous flirts.

MRS COSTELLO: I didn't hear what you said, Frederick. Probably just as well, as I can see you are intoxicated with the girl. Enough of this nonsense. I am going to lie down. You have revived my headache, you wretched boy. Come to my room this evening at eight sharp, and we will dine together.

WINTERBOURNE watches his aunt leave. As the lights go down on the terrace, WINTERBOURNE comes downstage and changes for the evening, continuing to address the audience.

WINTERBOURNE: My aunt has always harboured cast-iron prejudices against those poor mortals she deems her social inferiors. In spite of her harsh words about Miss Miller and her family, I am impatient to meet the young lady again: but I hardly know what reason I should give for my aunt's refusal to be introduced to her. It is indeed an embarrassing situation to be thrust into, and any attempt at an explanation will only stretch one's tact to the very limit.

The lights come up on a moonlit evening on the terrace.

It is 10 pm.

DAISY enters carrying a huge fan.

A small orchestra plays in the distance.

DAISY: Oh! It's you again. I have just spent the longest evening of my life!

WINTERBOURNE: Have you been all alone?

DAISY: I have been walking round with mother.

WINTERBOURNE: What have you been doing?

DAISY: Trying to get Randolph to go to bed. He's so annoying. He spends every minute trying to escape from mother and Eugenio.

WINTERBOURNE: Has your mother gone off to bed?

DAISY: No; she doesn't much like to going to bed. She doesn't sleep – not three hours. She says she doesn't know how she lives. I guess she sleeps more than she thinks. She was looking for Randolph too.

WINTERBOURNE: Doesn't he like going to bed?

DAISY: No.

WINTERBOURNE: Let's hope she will persuade him.

DAISY: She can talk to him until she's blue in the face, but it won't do any good. He won't listen to her.

WINTERBOURNE: What about Eugenio? Can't he handle Randolph?

DAISY: Randolph isn't afraid of him, so it's no good. I have been looking around for that lady you want to introduce me to. She's your aunt!

WINTERBOURNE: How did you learn that?

DAISY: I asked the chambermaid about her.

WINTERBOURNE: You did? And what did she tell you?

DAISY: That your aunt is very quiet – very *comme il faut*. She speaks to no one, never dines at the *table d'hôte*, and every two days she has a headache.

WINTERBOURNE: I guess that's a pretty accurate description of her.

DAISY: I think it's a lovely description, headache and all. I want to meet her ever so much. I know just what your aunt is like; I know I shall like her. She will be very exclusive. I like a lady to be exclusive. I'm dying to be exclusive myself.

WINTERBOURNE: Maybe you *are* exclusive.

DAISY: Well, I guess we are, mother and I. We don't speak to everyone – or they don't speak to us. I suppose it's about the same thing. Anyway, I shall be ever so glad to meet your aunt.

WINTERBOURNE: She would be most happy, but those headaches are always to be reckoned with.

DAISY: But I suppose she doesn't have one every day.

WINTERBOURNE: She tells me she does.

DAISY: She doesn't want to know me! Why don't you say so? You needn't be afraid! I'm not afraid!

WINTERBOURNE: My dear young lady, she knows no one.

DAISY: Why *should* she want to know me? (*Pause.*) Gracious, she *is* exclusive!

WINTERBOURNE: Where did you go this afternoon?

DAISY: Eugenio took us on a shopping trip. But I needn't have come here for the dresses. I'm sure they send all the pretty ones to New York; you see the most frightful dresses here. At home I have ever so many pretty dresses from Paris, and whenever I put on a Paris dress there, I feel as if I am in Europe. Look, there's mother. I guess she hasn't got my brother to go to bed yet.

WINTERBOURNE: Perhaps I had better leave you.

DAISY: Oh, no; come on!

WINTERBOURNE: Maybe your mother won't approve of my being with you.

DAISY: Mother doesn't like any of my gentlemen friends.

WINTERBOURNE: Why is that?

DAISY: She's downright timid. She always makes a fuss if I introduce a gentleman. But I *do* introduce them – almost always. I shouldn't think I was natural if I didn't.

WINTERBOURNE: Well, to introduce me, you must know my name. Frederick Forsyth Winterbourne.

DAISY: (*Laughing.*) I can't say all that! I'll never remember it.

MRS MILLER enters. She is elegantly dressed, and has enormous diamond earrings, but the effect is marred by an unmatching shawl over her shoulders, which she hugs to keep out the chill. She is a frail, nervous woman, seemingly anxious about her health.

Mother! I want you to meet Mr Frederick Forsyth Winterbourne. Mr Winterbourne, my mother. What are you doing poking around here?

MRS MILLER: Well, I don't know.

DAISY: I shouldn't think you'd want that old shawl of mine!

MRS MILLER: Well – I do!

DAISY: Did you get Randolph to go to bed?

MRS MILLER: No, I couldn't make him. He wants to talk to the waiter. He *likes* to talk to that waiter.

WINTERBOURNE: I have the pleasure of knowing your son, Mrs Miller. We met this morning in the garden. He is quite a character. I'm afraid I was inveigled into allowing him a lump of sugar.

MRS MILLER: He knows perfectly well I disapprove of him eating sugar lumps. He is ruining his teeth. I am finding it very difficult to control him. I really believe he will be quite toothless by the time we get back to Schenectady.

DAISY: It isn't so bad as it was at Dover...

WINTERBOURNE: And what occurred at Dover?

DAISY: He didn't go to bed at all. He sat up all night – in the public parlour.

MRS MILLER: It was half past twelve when *I* gave up.

WINTERBOURNE: Does he sleep much during the day?

DAISY: I guess he doesn't sleep much at all.

MRS MILLER: I wish he just *would.* It seems as if he couldn't.

DAISY: I think he's real tiresome.

MRS MILLER: Daisy Miller! I shouldn't think you'd want to talk against your own brother!

DAISY: Randolph *is* tiresome, mother.

MRS MILLER: He's only nine.

DAISY: He wouldn't go up to that castle, so I'm going up there with Mr Winterbourne.

WINTERBOURNE: Your daughter has kindly allowed me the honour of being her guide. I suggested that you might like to come too.

DAISY: But I explained, mother, about your dyspepsia, and you not liking to drive around in the afternoon.

MRS MILLER: I guess you will go by train.

WINTERBOURNE: Yes; or on the steamer.

MRS MILLER: Well, of course, I don't know. I have never been to that old castle.

WINTERBOURNE: It's a pity you won't come with us.

MRS MILLER: We've been thinking ever so much about going ever since we arrived here but it seems as if we couldn't. Of course Daisy – she wants to go round everywhere, but there's a lady here – I don't know her name – she says she shouldn't think we'd want to see the castles *here*; she thinks we'd want to wait till we get to Italy. Of course, we only want to see the important ones. We visited several in England.

WINTERBOURNE: Ah yes! In England there are very fine castles. Which ones did you see?

MRS MILLER: Windsor Castle, of course. We went to Warwick Castle as well, and a few others, but I forget now. Everything becomes blurred after a while. We are always on the move.

WINTERBOURNE: I can assure you that Chillon is well worth a visit.

MRS MILLER: If Daisy feels up to it – it seems there is nothing she wouldn't undertake.

WINTERBOURNE: I'm pretty sure she'll enjoy it! Will you not come with us?

MRS MILLER looks at him askance, ignoring the question.

MRS MILLER: I guess she had better go alone.

DAISY: Mr Winterbourne! Don't you want to take me out in a boat?

WINTERBOURNE: Now?

DAISY: Of course!

MRS MILLER: Annie Miller!

WINTERBOURNE: I beg you, madam, do let her go!

MRS MILLER: I shouldn't think she'd want to. I should think she'd rather go indoors.

DAISY: I'm sure Mr Winterbourne wants to take me. He's so awfully devoted!

WINTERBOURNE: I will row you over to Chillon, under the stars!

DAISY: I don't believe it!

MRS MILLER: Well!

WINTERBOURNE: There are half a dozen boats moored at that landing-place. If you'll do me the honour to accept my arm, we will go and select one of them.

DAISY: I like a gentleman to be formal!

WINTERBOURNE: I assure you it's a formal offer. But I'm afraid you're teasing me.

MRS MILLER: I think not, sir.

WINTERBOURNE: Do, then, let me take you for a row.

DAISY: It's quite lovely, the way you say that!

WINTERBOURNE: It will be still more lovely to do it.

DAISY: (*Laughing but not moving.*) Yes, it would be lovely.

MRS MILLER: I think you'd better find out what time it is.

DAISY: I don't care what time it is. I'm going with Mr Winterbourne. This very minute.

MRS MILLER: I think you had better not go out in a boat, Daisy, at this time of night. What will Eugenio say?

DAISY: He won't think it's proper. Eugenio doesn't think anything's proper.

MRS MILLER: Perhaps he's right, Daisy. I don't think you should go, although I'm sure Mr Winterbourne is a very respectable gentleman. It just doesn't seem right at this late hour.

DAISY: I hoped you'd make a fuss! I don't want to go now.

WINTERBOURNE: I shall make a fuss if you don't go.

DAISY: That's all I want – a little fuss.

MRS MILLER: Come along, Daisy, we must go to bed.

DAISY: Good night. I hope you're disappointed, or disgusted, or something!

WINTERBOURNE: (*Taking her hand.*) I'm puzzled.

DAISY: Well; I hope it won't keep you awake!

DAISY and MRS MILLER leave.

WINTERBOURNE is still for a moment, then turns to the audience.

WINTERBOURNE: What a baffling young girl she is!

He is about to continue but DAISY rushes in breathless.

DAISY: You can still take me to the castle tomorrow. Can we go by the little steamer?

She doesn't wait for an answer and exits.

WINTERBOURNE turns to the audience.

WINTERBOURNE: I am more than disconcerted, I am bewildered, by Daisy's proneness to a sudden change of mood, not to say a change of mind. I think I'll take a walk down by the lake to clear my thoughts about her. In spite of her odd behaviour, I am looking forward with pleasure to our trip to the Château. (*Exits.*)

The next day. Bright sunshine. Noise of steam boats.

MRS COSTELLO comes into the garden and sits at a table under an umbrella. She takes a letter from her bag and reads it.

A WAITER appears and she orders tea.

MRS COSTELLO: (*To the WAITER.*) Garçon! Je voudrais du thé.

WAITER: Certainement, madame. Avec du lait ou nature?

MRS COSTELLO: Nature, s'il vous plaît.

The WAITER leaves and MRS COSTELLO calls after him.

N'oubliez pas le passoire.

She returns to her letter and looks up as WINTERBOURNE enters.

WINTERBOURNE: *Passoire.* That always strikes me as a very grand word for a tea strainer!

MRS COSTELLO: Ah, Frederick, I was hoping to see you. I've invited your cousin to join me for the summer. She writes to say she's arriving next week.

WINTERBOURNE: (*Slightly irritated.*) Which cousin is that, aunt?

MRS COSTELLO: Alice Stepney.

WINTERBOURNE: I don't believe I've ever met her.

MRS COSTELLO: She's your father's cousin's daughter. A pretty young thing, you'll like her. We are surrounded by objects of interest here, and we'll depend upon you to be our guide.

WINTERBOURNE: My dear aunt, I'm afraid I don't know much about the surrounding objects!

MRS COSTELLO: Don't be ridiculous, Frederick, of course you know about them. Alice has a great desire to climb a mountain – and to examine a glacier.

WINTERBOURNE: You should go to Zermatt. You're in the midst of glaciers there.

MRS COSTELLO: We shall be delighted to go – under your escort. She doesn't rush about the world alone, like a certain American girl I could mention.

WINTERBOURNE: Miss Miller is not rushing around alone, aunt. She is with her mother and the courier.

MRS COSTELLO: Nevertheless, she gives the impression that she does what she likes. Alice has been brought up like the young ladies in Geneva. Her education was surrounded with every precaution.

WINTERBOURNE: The best education, surely, is seeing the world a little.

MRS COSTELLO: That's precisely what I wish her to do. When we have finished Zermatt, we'll come back to Interlaken and Lucerne.

WINTERBOURNE: I'm not sure, aunt, if I will have the time to escort you. I have to return to Geneva.

MRS COSTELLO: Nonsense, Frederick. If you are able to find time to take that little girl to the Château de Chillon, the least you can do is escort your own cousin on some excursions.

WINTERBOURNE: She's a very distant cousin, Aunt.

MRS COSTELLO: Distant or not, I shall expect you to do your duty, Frederick. By the way, have you been to the castle yet?

WINTERBOURNE: I'm waiting for Miss Miller to join me at two o'clock.

MRS COSTELLO: Here? You've made an appointment to meet her here? (*She gets up to leave.*) You're going with her all alone?

WINTERBOURNE: All alone.

MRS COSTELLO: And that's the young person you wanted me to know. I'm very much disappointed in you, Frederick. (*She holds her hand to her head.*) I can feel I am about to have a headache. I'm going to my room.

WINTERBOURNE: I'll tell them to make sure you're not disturbed.

MRS COSTELLO: I'm glad to see you still have some manners.

She exits quickly.

DAISY appears with a huge hat and parasol and buttoning her gloves.

DAISY: Was that your aunt?

WINTERBOURNE: Yes, it was.

DAISY: Did she see me? Is that why she left so quickly?

WINTERBOURNE: No, I don't think she saw you. She had one of her headaches coming on.

WAITER enters with tray of tea.

WAITER: Voilà le thé pour Madame, monsieur.

WINTERBOURNE: Je regrette mais Madame n'a plus besoin du thé. Elle a un de ses maux de tête.

WAITER: (*Looks at tray, shrugs.*) Très bien, monsieur. (*Exits.*)

DAISY: So she really does have headaches almost every day! I thought you were making that up, to protect me. Were you having an argument with her? Is that why she left so quickly?

WINTERBOURNE: We were having something of a disagreement, yes.

DAISY: What about?

WINTERBOURNE: My dear Miss Miller. It was a family matter.

DAISY: Oh. I'd rather hoped it was about me. I haven't kept you waiting too long, have I, Mr Winterbourne? I was afraid you wouldn't wait for me.

WINTERBOURNE: I don't know what gave you that impression.

DAISY: Half the time they don't wait – the gentlemen.

WINTERBOURNE: That's in America, perhaps. But over here they always wait.

DAISY: I haven't had much experience over here.

WINTERBOURNE: I am glad to hear it.

DAISY: Mother has had a bad night, and didn't want me to leave. I told her Eugenio and Randolph are perfectly capable of looking after her.

WINTERBOURNE: Surely Eugenio doesn't sit with your mother?

DAISY: Not always, because he likes to go out. He's got a great many friends; he's awfully popular. And, after all, you know, poor mother isn't very amusing. He stays with her all he can: he says he didn't expect that so much when he came.

WINTERBOURNE: I should think not! I haven't known you very long, but allow me to give you a piece of advice. Do not gossip with your courier!

A steamer's hooter is heard.

DAISY: He's quite entertaining. I get so bored being with mother and Randolph. He knows almost as much as you do, Mr Winterbourne!

EUGENIO appears.

EUGENIO: Mademoiselle, your mother requests that you will come to her.

DAISY: I don't believe a word of it!

EUGENIO: You should not do me the injustice to doubt my honour.

DAISY: Mother knows exactly where I am and what I am going to do.

EUGENIO: I think Mademoiselle will find that Madame is very anxious.

DAISY: My dear Eugenio, Madame will be perfectly all right with you.

EUGENIO: I take the liberty of advising Mademoiselle not to go to the castle.

DAISY: I suppose you don't think it's proper. (*To WINTERBOURNE.*) Eugenio doesn't think anything's proper.

EUGENIO: Does Mademoiselle propose to go alone?

DAISY: Oh, no, with this gentleman!

EUGENIO: As Mademoiselle pleases!

Steamer's hooter is heard again.

WINTERBOURNE: The steamer's leaving in ten minutes, we'd better go.

DAISY: How lovely! You've booked the little steamer. I hope you don't mind not going by train.

WINTERBOURNE and DAISY exit.

Distant sound of steamer leaving.

MRS MILLER enters.

MRS MILLER: (*Watching from the edge of the lake.*) I do hope I've done the right thing, letting Daisy go alone with Mr Winterbourne. I don't know what Mr Miller would say.

EUGENIO: Madame, I had hoped to show you the castle myself. No Swiss historic monument is better known. It has become a symbol of our country.

MRS MILLER: Oh, my!

EUGENIO: Perhaps a little walk along the lake before luncheon?

MRS MILLER: Oh, do you think so, Eugenio? I wonder if I'll be up to it? My dyspepsia kept me up all night. Where is Randolph?

EUGENIO: He may be down by the lake, or talking to the waiter.

MRS MILLER: Oh, look, there he is! (*Calling.*) Randolph!

They exit.

Scene changes to deck of steamer. Sound of ship's engines, hooters etc.

DAISY and WINTERBOURNE enter.

DAISY: Come on Mr Winterbourne, let's stay up on deck. I like to feel the wind in my hair. (*Laughing.*) What on *earth* are you so solemn about?

WINTERBOURNE: *Am* I solemn? I had an idea I was grinning from ear to ear.

DAISY: You look as if you were taking me to a prayer meeting or a funeral. If that's a grin, your ears are very close together.

WINTERBOURNE: Do you want me to dance a hornpipe on the deck?

DAISY: (*Laughing.*) Pray do, and I'll carry round your hat. It will pay the expenses of our journey!

WINTERBOURNE: I never was better pleased in my life.

DAISY: I like to hear you say those things. You're a strange mixture!

The ship's telegraph rings and the engines gather speed as they move off.

I am so glad I persuaded you to take me by steamer. I have a passion for steamboats. There is usually such a lovely breeze on the water, and you see so many people. Oh! Would you believe it? There's that English lady I was telling you about. The one we met on the train.

She runs away from WINTERBOURNE and calls and waves.

Miss Featherstone, Miss Featherstone.

WINTERBOURNE waits impatiently.

She didn't see me, or didn't want to see me. I don't know which. But never mind.

As DAISY leans over the rail, WINTERBOURNE turns to the audience.

WINTERBOURNE: If I had expected Daisy to be in a nervous flutter, I was wrong. My own awkwardness is much greater. I was afraid she might talk and laugh too loudly, my aunt's words about her commonness still ringing in my ears. Daisy is in the brightest of spirits. I notice people are watching her, and I take pleasure in this. The journey passes all too quickly.

The boat slows down with a backwash of propellers, the sound of chains and the ship's telegraph as it stops. Lights up on the Château de Chillon as they walk downstage.

DAISY: Are we really here?

WINTERBOURNE: (*Amused at her excitement.*) Yes, we are really here.

DAISY: It was so exciting crossing that little wooden bridge! I tried to imagine what the prisoners must have felt when they crossed over it.

WINTERBOURNE: Let me tell you about the Château.

DAISY: Don't tell me too much, or my head will start to spin! It is all so wonderful. Look at that tower. Can we go up there? And all those turrets, I want to go in all of them, and where does that archway lead to? Are those the stairs down to the dungeon? Come on, Mr Winterbourne, let's go and have...

WINTERBOURNE: (*Interrupts her.*) Slow down, Miss Miller! Stay here for a moment or two, and drink in the atmosphere. You'll enjoy the experience all the more if you take your time.

DAISY: Oh, very well then. I suppose you are going to recite some more poetry!

WINTERBOURNE: (*Laughing.*) As a matter of fact I was. How did you guess?

DAISY: You were putting on your poetry voice. Keats again?

WINTERBOURNE: No, Byron this time. Lord Byron wrote a famous poem about a very brave man who was locked up in this place: it's called 'The Prisoner of Chillon'.

DAISY: Well, I certainly know who Lord Byron was. Didn't he die in a duel?

WINTERBOURNE: No, he died from a fever, probably malaria, at a place called Missolonghi, fighting for Greece against the Turks.

DAISY: Not in a duel? Are you sure?

WINTERBOURNE: Yes.

DAISY: What a pity. Dying in a duel seems so much more romantic than dying from malaria!

DAISY starts to giggle, her laughter is infectious and sets WINTERBOURNE off too. Out of the laughter he takes on an heroic pose and gives quite a performance.

WINTERBOURNE:
Chillon! thy prison is a holy place,
And thy sad floor an altar, – for 'twas trod,
Until his very steps have left a trace
Worn, as if thy cold pavement were a sod,
By Bonnivard! – may none those marks efface!
For they appeal from tyranny to God.

DAISY: (*Laughs and claps her hands.*) You are so smart. Who was Bonnivard?

WINTERBOURNE: François de Bonnivard was the Prior of St Victor, near Geneva; he backed a revolt by the people of Geneva against Charles III of Savoy. He was imprisoned here in the Sixteenth Century. Bonnivard became a symbol of the people's struggle for liberty.

DAISY: I think I know how he must have felt, imprisoned and longing to be free! Will you say the rest of that poem to me?

WINTERBOURNE: I will say any poetry you like.

DAISY: Then we will have to spend a great deal of time together, won't we? (*She looks at him to see his reaction.*) When was the castle built? It seems very ancient.

WINTERBOURNE: It was built in 1238, although some parts go back to 1160.

DAISY: Well! I hope you know enough! I never saw a man that knew so much! Look at this pretty courtyard. And the balcony up there.

WINTERBOURNE: It reminds me of *Romeo and Juliet.*

DAISY: Oh! we studied *Romeo and Juliet* at school.

O Romeo, Romeo! wherefore art thou Romeo?

WINTERBOURNE: Now *I* am impressed!

DAISY: I like to impress you!

Give me my Romeo; and, when he shall die,
Take him and cut him out in little stars,
And he will make the face of heaven so fine
That all the world will be in love with night
And pay no worship to the garish sun.

Every time I look at the stars I think of Romeo. It makes the night more exciting, don't you think?

WINTERBOURNE: I must confess I've never thought about it, but yes, you're right, it is a powerful image. I will always think of *you* from now on, when I look at the stars.

DAISY: I'll like that. I think you suppose I'm uneducated. In some ways, maybe I am, but sometimes, you see, I can surprise you! Shall I go up on the balcony, and we can play the balcony scene together?

WINTERBOURNE: I don't know the lines as well as you do.

DAISY: I will learn some Keats and Byron, and you can learn the balcony scene, and next time we meet we can test each other.

WINTERBOURNE: That's quite a challenge, Miss Miller.

DAISY: Have you brought other young ladies here?

WINTERBOURNE: (*Taken aback.*) I brought a group of friends here once, and among them were some young ladies, yes.

DAISY looks quizzically at him.

DAISY: Was there a *special* young lady?

WINTERBOURNE: No, there wasn't a *special* young lady. Now take a look at that huge vaulted ceiling, isn't that fine?

DAISY: You are changing the subject. (*Laughs.*) I'll bet it was cold in here then. Even with that enormous fireplace. What's that above it?

WINTERBOURNE: That is the coat-of-arms of the Catholic Dukes of Savoy. It became their favourite summer residence. The main reason for this was its strategic position.

DAISY: What do you mean?

WINTERBOURNE: From here you can see over the mountains – (*He puts his hand gently on her arm and guides her to the window.*) – that's the road to Italy. They could keep watch from here. Now if you look out of this window you will see –

DAISY: Lake Geneva! It's very romantic, isn't it?

They stand for a moment close together.

Tell me about your parents. And why you are living in Geneva.

WINTERBOURNE: Both my parents are dead, I'm afraid. My mother died when I was quite young, and my father when I started university.

DAISY starts to speak but WINTERBOURNE cuts her off.

It's a long time ago now. I went to school in Geneva, where my father was working in the American Consulate, and then I decided to stay on at the university, and I've been in Geneva ever since.

DAISY: Do you never feel the urge to go back to America?

WINTERBOURNE: I think Europe suits me better.

DAISY: Have you any brothers or sisters? I sometimes think I would like to have a sister, instead of that irritating little brother.

WINTERBOURNE: But Randolph's just a normal, inquisitive, lively little boy. And I think he's quite entertaining.

DAISY pulls a face.

By the way, you ask a great many questions!

DAISY: If I don't ask questions, how am I to find out more about you? You are so... stiff. I want to know *all* about you.

WINTERBOURNE: No, I don't have any siblings. Just cousins.

DAISY: I wish I could persuade you to come and teach Randolph.

WINTERBOURNE: I'm afraid I have other things to do.

DAISY: Other things to do? I don't believe a word of it! What do you mean? You are not in business, are you?

WINTERBOURNE: No, I am not in business, but I have engagements in Geneva, which I cannot break.

DAISY: I don't believe it!

WINTERBOURNE: In fact, I have to leave the day after tomorrow.

DAISY: You don't mean to say you are going back to Geneva so soon.

WINTERBOURNE: I'm afraid so.

DAISY: Mr Winterbourne, I think you're horrid. Horrid, horrid, horrid.

WINTERBOURNE: Don't say such dreadful things!

DAISY: I've half a mind to leave you here and go straight back to the hotel alone.

WINTERBOURNE: I will take you back immediately, if that's what you want.

DAISY: I suppose you have some mysterious charmer waiting for you in Geneva.

WINTERBOURNE: I have nothing of the sort, I can assure you.

DAISY: Does she never allow you more than three days at a time? Doesn't she give you a vacation in summer? I suppose, if you stay another day, she'll come after you in the boat.

WINTERBOURNE: Miss Miller, you are being ridiculous.

DAISY: Do stay until Friday, and I will go down to the landing to see her arrive. I would like to see what this charmer looks like!

WINTERBOURNE: Miss Miller, you must stop this nonsense!

DAISY: I will stop teasing you, Mr Winterbourne, if you promise to come to Rome this winter.

WINTERBOURNE: That is not a difficult promise to make. My aunt has taken an apartment in Rome for the winter, and has already asked me to come and see her. And will you promise to let me take you to the house where Keats lived?

DAISY: I promise. But I don't want you to come for your aunt; I want you to come for me.

Music. The lights fade on the two figures in the castle.

End of Act One.

ACT TWO

The stage is dark.

WINTERBOURNE steps forward into a pool of light. He has a letter in his hand.

WINTERBOURNE: I returned to Geneva the day after my excursion with Daisy to the castle. Aunt Alice wrote me from Rome where she was established in her apartment near the Spanish Steps. (*He reads.*) 'Frederick, those people you were so devoted to last summer at Vevey have turned up here, in Rome, courier and all. They seem to have made several acquaintances, but the courier continues to be most *intime*. The young lady, however, is also very close with various third-rate Italians, with whom she rackets about in a way that makes much talk. Don't forget to bring me that pretty novel of Cherbuliez's – *Paule Méré* – and don't come later than the twenty-third!' So here I am.

Lights up on MRS COSTELLO's apartment. The sound of distant church bells.

I am rather dreading this encounter with my dear aunt, and would much rather have seen Daisy first.

MRS COSTELLO enters.

MRS COSTELLO: Did you remember to bring that French novel with you, Frederick?

WINTERBOURNE: *Paule Méré*? Yes, of course.

WINTERBOURNE hands it to her.

MRS COSTELLO: Thank you, dear boy. I thought you might forget.

WINTERBOURNE: You didn't give me a chance to forget! And how was Alice?

MRS COSTELLO: (*Irritated.*) Alice who?

WINTERBOURNE: Cousin Alice, in London. You invited her to stay with you. From Stepney. You must remember.

MRS COSTELLO: Not *from* Stepney. She is a Stepney. Alice Stepney. You know that perfectly well. She turned out to be very plain, I'm afraid. Worthy, but plain. She fractured her ankle on a glacier, and went back to Philadelphia.

WINTERBOURNE: That was unfortunate.

MRS COSTELLO: (*Ignoring him.*) I suppose you are going to visit those dreadful people.

WINTERBOURNE: Yes. I promised Miss Miller I would visit her in Rome, and I'm not in the habit of breaking my promises.

MRS COSTELLO: If you desire to keep up the acquaintance, you're very welcome. Of course – a man may know everyone. Men are welcome to the privilege!

WINTERBOURNE: What exactly *is* it that the Millers do, that causes such concern?

MRS COSTELLO: The girl tears about alone with her foreigners. As to what happens further, you must apply elsewhere for information. She has picked up half a dozen of the regular Roman fortune-hunters and she takes them about to people's houses. When she comes to a party she brings with her a young man with a good deal of manner and a wonderful moustache.

WINTERBOURNE: And where's the mother?

MRS COSTELLO: I haven't the least idea. They're very dreadful people.

WINTERBOURNE: They're ignorant, I grant you, but they are not 'bad'. Just innocent.

MRS COSTELLO: They are hopelessly vulgar. Whether or not being hopelessly vulgar is being 'bad' is a question for the metaphysicians. The Millers are bad enough to dislike, at any rate; and for this short life that is quite enough.

She exits.

Down on MRS COSTELLO's light.

WINTERBOURNE steps forward.

WINTERBOURNE: While travelling to Rome I had indulged the idea that I would see Daisy looking out of an old Roman window waiting impatiently for me to arrive. But the reality is different. After what my aunt has told me, I have decided not to hurry round and see Daisy as I had planned. Instead, I shall call on an old friend.

Lights come up on MRS WALKER's apartment.

MRS WALKER: Freddie, what a pleasant surprise! I hadn't realised you were already in Rome.

WINTERBOURNE: Did you not get my letter?

MRS WALKER: Yes, I did. I've been so busy, I'm afraid I hadn't really registered when you said you were arriving. Do forgive me. It's very good to see you.

WINTERBOURNE: I suppose you've been preoccupied with all your charity work, as usual.

MRS WALKER: You make it sound awfully dull, Freddie. In truth, I've been having a very jolly time. You know

how Rome sparkles in the winter. Concerts, ballet,
opera, not to mention all the exhibitions. You have to
see the splendid new gallery in the Villa Borghese.

WINTERBOURNE: Perhaps you will come with me... I
have to talk to you, Emily.

MRS WALKER: What about? You look so serious. Are
you still studying in Geneva?

WINTERBOURNE: Sometimes. I go to the university and
use the library there, but most of the time I am writing.

MRS WALKER: What are you writing?

WINTERBOURNE: I'm doing travel pieces about Europe
for an American newspaper.

MRS WALKER: And what about the young ladies? One
or two of them seemed to be quite infatuated with you
when I last saw you in Geneva.

WINTERBOURNE: I'd like your advice, Emily. Last
summer in Vevey I became acquainted with an
interesting young American girl, she...

A SERVANT appears and announces:

SERVANT: Madame Mila.

The sound of voices and DAISY and MRS MILLER enter.

DAISY: Well, I declare! Mr Winterbourne.

WINTERBOURNE: (*Surprised.*) I told you I should come,
you know.

DAISY: Well – I didn't believe it.

WINTERBOURNE: (*Laughing.*) I am much obliged to
you.

DAISY: (*To MRS WALKER.*) We met in Switzerland last
summer. Mr Winterbourne was very kind to me. He

took me to the Château de Chillon. Do you know
Switzerland, Mrs Walker?

MRS WALKER: Yes, my dear, very well. My husband
was the American ambassador in Geneva. Our children
went to school there.

DAISY: So did Mr Winterbourne! You must have known
him when he was a little boy.

MRS WALKER: Very well indeed. Won't you sit down,
Mrs Miller?

MRS MILLER: How very kind of you.

WINTERBOURNE: Mrs Walker took me under her wing
after my mother died.

DAISY: You might have come to see me earlier, Mr
Winterbourne.

WINTERBOURNE: My dear young lady, I arrived in
Rome only yesterday.

DAISY: I don't believe that! We have a beautiful apartment
in an hotel near the Spanish Steps. I haven't bumped
into your aunt, though. (*To WINTERBOURNE.*) You did
say her apartment was near the Spanish Steps, did you
not?

WINTERBOURNE: Yes, it is. But, as I told you, my aunt
doesn't get out much.

DAISY: You should just see *our* apartment. It's all gold on
the walls, and bigger than this place. We've got splendid
rooms. Eugenio says they are the best in Rome.
Everything you told me about Rome is true. I'm so glad
we are near the Spanish Steps. I dazzle everyone with
my knowledge, not letting on, of course, that I got it all
from you.

WINTERBOURNE: I'm flattered that you remember what I told you. But I hope you haven't been to see Keats's house yet.

DAISY: Of course not! I keep my promises.

MRS WALKER: (*To MRS MILLER.*) Mrs Miller, I trust you have been well since you arrived in Rome.

MRS MILLER: Not very well, ma'am.

DAISY: Mother's still got the dyspepsia. Everyone in our family seems to get it except me! Father, mother and even Randolph.

MRS MILLER: I suffer from the liver. I think it's the climate. It's less bracing than Schenectady, especially in the winter season.

DAISY: Nonsense, mother! It has nothing to do with the climate. You get dyspepsia wherever you are.

MRS MILLER: I don't care what you say, Daisy... I don't know whether you are aware, Mrs Walker, that we reside in Schenectady.

MRS WALKER: Indeed!

MRS MILLER: I was saying to Daisy, that I hadn't found anyone like my Dr Davis, and I don't believe I shall.

MRS WALKER: The doctors in Rome are renowned for their expertise, Mrs Miller, you need have no fear.

MRS MILLER: Up in Schenectady Dr Davis stands first; he's at the very top. They think everything of him. He has so much to do, and yet there was nothing he wouldn't do for *me*. He said he never saw anything like my dyspepsia, but he was sure he could cure it. I'm sure there was nothing he wouldn't try, and I didn't care what he did to me if he only brought me relief. He was about to try something new when we left.

MRS WALKER: I'm very sorry to hear about your condition, Mrs Miller.

MRS MILLER: Mr Miller wanted Daisy to see Europe for herself, but I couldn't help writing the other day that I supposed it was all right for Daisy, but that I didn't know as I *could* get on much longer without Dr Davis. It affects my sleep, you know. I don't know what I'm going to do.

WINTERBOURNE: (*Changing the subject.*) You must be pleased to be in Rome.

MRS MILLER: I must say I'm very disappointed.

MRS WALKER: Disappointed? I'm sorry to hear that.

MRS MILLER: We had heard so much about it. I suppose we had heard too much. We had been led to expect something different.

WINTERBOURNE: Wait a little, and you will become very fond of Rome.

MRS MILLER: Randolph hates it more every day. He just wants to go home.

DAISY: Mother; don't burden Mr Winterbourne too much.

MRS MILLER: We have seen places in Europe that I should put a long way before Rome.

MRS WALKER: I *am* surprised.

MRS MILLER: There's Zürich, up there in the mountains. I think Zürich's real lovely; and we hadn't heard half so much about it.

WINTERBOURNE: At least your daughter is enjoying Rome?

MRS MILLER: Oh, Daisy! She's quite carried away! It's on account of the society – she thinks the society's splendid. She goes round everywhere; she has made a great number of acquaintances. She knows a great many gentlemen. She thinks there's nothing like Rome! Of course, it's a great deal pleasanter for a young lady if she knows plenty of gentlemen.

DAISY: (*To WINTERBOURNE.*) I shall tell Mrs Walker how mean you were.

WINTERBOURNE: And what is the evidence you will offer?

DAISY: Why, you were *awfully* mean at Vevey. You wouldn't do anything. You wouldn't stay on there when I asked you.

WINTERBOURNE: My dear young lady, have I come all the way to Rome, not even stopping off at Bologna and Florence, to encounter your reproaches?

DAISY: Just hear him say that! Did you ever hear anything so quaint?

MRS WALKER: So quaint, my dear?

DAISY: Yes, quaint, you know what I mean. Mrs Walker, I want to tell you about something. You know, I'm coming to your party.

MRS WALKER: I am delighted to hear it.

DAISY: I've got a lovely dress.

MRS WALKER: I am very sure of that.

DAISY: But I want to ask you a favour, permission to bring a friend.

MRS WALKER: (*Smiling at MRS MILLER.*) I shall be happy to see any of your friends.

MRS MILLER: Oh, they are not my friends. I never spoke to them!

DAISY: It's an intimate friend of mine – Mr Giovanelli.

MRS WALKER: (*Glancing at WINTERBOURNE.*)
I shall be glad to see Mr Giovanelli.

DAISY: He's the handsomest man in the world – except
Mr Winterbourne! Mr Giovanelli knows plenty of
Italians, but he wants to know some Americans. He
thinks ever so much of Americans.

MRS WALKER: I'm relieved to hear it!

DAISY: He's tremendously clever! He's perfectly lovely!

MRS MILLER: I guess, Daisy, it's time we went back to
the hotel.

DAISY: You may go back to the hotel, mother, but I'm
going to take a walk. I am going to the Pincio.

MRS WALKER: Alone, my dear, at this hour? I don't
think it's safe.

MRS MILLER: Neither do I. You'll get the fever as sure as
you live. Remember what Dr Davis told you!

DAISY: (*Kissing MRS WALKER.*) Mrs Walker, you are
too perfect. I'm not going alone; I am going to meet a
friend.

MRS MILLER: Your friend won't keep you from getting
the fever.

MRS WALKER: Is it Mr Giovanelli?

DAISY: (*Smiling at WINTERBOURNE.*) Mr Giovanelli
– the beautiful Giovanelli.

MRS WALKER: My dear, don't walk off to the Pincio at
this hour to meet an Italian, however beautiful he is.

MRS MILLER: He speaks English.

DAISY: Gracious me! I don't want to do anything improper. There's an easy way to settle it. If Mr Winterbourne were as polite as he pretends he would offer to walk me! The Pincio is only a few minutes away.

WINTERBOURNE: Of course I will accompany you. Please take my arm.

DAISY: Mother, don't wait dinner for me. I may have other arrangements.

MRS MILLER: What shall I say to Eugenio? He will be most upset.

DAISY: Say what you like. Eugenio is not my keeper.

MRS WALKER: Let me accompany you to your carriage, Mrs Miller. (*She takes her by the arm.*)

MRS MILLER: Perhaps, after all, you had better give me the name of one of your doctors.

They exit together leaving WINTERBOURNE and DAISY.

A SERVANT brings WINTERBOURNE his hat, gloves and stick.

DAISY takes his arm as they come down stage.

They walk to the pincio.

DAISY: Why haven't you been to see me? You can't get out of that.

WINTERBOURNE: I have already told you I have only just stepped off the train.

DAISY: You must have stayed in the train a good while after it stopped! I suppose you were asleep. You have had time to go and see Mrs Walker.

WINTERBOURNE: I knew Mrs Walker –

DAISY: In Geneva. Yes, I know. Well, you knew me in Vevey. That's just as good. So you ought to have come. We are going to stay all winter – if we don't die of the fever; and I guess we'll have to stay *then*! Rome is even better than I thought.

WINTERBOURNE: In what way?

DAISY: I thought it would be fearfully quiet. I was sure it would be awfully poky, and that we should be going round all the time with one of those dreadful old men that explain about pictures and things, just as you did at the Château de Chillon (*She looks at him mischievously.*) – but we only had about a week of that, and now I'm enjoying myself.

WINTERBOURNE: I thought you enjoyed yourself at the Château de Chillon.

DAISY: Oh, yes, I did. I don't mean to sound ungrateful. Well, now I know ever so many people, and they are all so charming. The society's extremely select. There are all kinds – English, and Germans and Italians. I like the English best. I like their style of conversation… But there are some lovely Americans too. There's something or other every day. Not much dancing, but then I never thought dancing was everything. I love conversation. I guess I shall have plenty at Mrs Walker's – her rooms are so small. It's a pity though that you can't walk in Rome without everyone staring so.

WINTERBOURNE: Miss Miller…

DAISY: (*Interrupts him.*) And here we are in the Pincio already. Do you remember you told me about the Pincio? I wonder where Mr Giovanelli might be!

WINTERBOURNE: I certainly shall not help you to find him.

DAISY: Then I shall find him without you. You don't seem to like anything I do. It's hard to know what you do like.

WINTERBOURNE: I'm only trying to protect you from making a mistake.

DAISY: You've got such peculiar tastes. It must be from your foreign education. Well, I haven't had a foreign education, and I don't see I'm any the worse for that. If I'd had a foreign education I might as well give up! I shouldn't be able to breathe for fear I was breathing wrong. There seem to be so many ways over here. Look! There's Mr Giovanelli, leaning against that tree. He's staring at the women in the carriages; did you ever see anything so cool?

WINTERBOURNE: Do you mean to speak to that man?

DAISY: Of course I do. You don't suppose I mean to communicate by signs?

WINTERBOURNE: Pray, understand then, that I intend to remain with you.

DAISY: I don't like the way you say that.

WINTERBOURNE: I beg your pardon if I have expressed myself too forcefully, but it is out of respect for you.

DAISY: I have never allowed a gentleman to dictate to me, or to interfere with anything I do.

WINTERBOURNE: You should sometimes listen to a gentleman – the right one, that is.

DAISY: Is Mr Giovanelli the right one?

WINTERBOURNE: No, he's not the right one. He is not a gentleman, he is only a clever imitation of one.

DAISY: Nevertheless, I am going to join him.

GIOVANELLI approaches them. He bows to DAISY and WINTERBOURNE and kisses DAISY's hand.

GIOVANELLI: How can I thank you for granting me this supreme satisfaction?

DAISY: That's a very fine way to describe a walk on the Pincio, Mr Giovanelli. This is Mr Winterbourne. Mr Winterbourne, Mr Giovanelli.

They shake hands politely.

Mr Winterbourne kindly escorted me from Mrs Walker's. She's given me her permission to bring you to her party. We must practise your songs. (*To WINTERBOURNE.*) He has such a beautiful voice. Bellissimo!

GIOVANELLI: (*Smiles.*) *Grazie tante*, Signorina.

DAISY: Mother is not expecting me back to dinner.

GIOVANELLI: You've consented to my little fantasy?

DAISY: (*Looking at WINTERBOURNE who has moved to one side.*) Of dining with you? Yes.

GIOVANELLI: You are a person of delicious surprises! The other day you would not listen to such an idea.

DAISY: I don't remember the other day: all I know is that I'll go now. Where are you going to take me?

GIOVANELLI: To the *Falcone*.

DAISY: Is that a restaurant?

GIOVANELLI: Near the Piazza Navona. It's delightful. You will adore it, Signorina.

WINTERBOURNE turns to the audience as GIOVANELLI and DAISY continue their conversation.

WINTERBOURNE: I'd guess he's a cavaliere avvocato, or minor lawyer, by profession, seemingly respectable, but I doubt if he moves in the best circles. He speaks English very cleverly and I imagine he's learnt it from his acquaintance with a great many American heiresses. His manners are impeccable. Although he has not counted upon a party of three, he keeps his temper and is politeness itself.

As WINTERBOURNE turns back to them, we hear DAISY and GIOVANELLI once again.

DAISY: (*Laughing.*) Can we throw a coin in the Trevi fountain? It's on the way, isn't it? I want to make a wish.

GIOVANELLI: Oh, yes! You must make a wish, otherwise you will not return, Signorina.

DAISY: I mean to come back. I will come back.

GIOVANELLI: You make me very happy!

DAISY: By going to eat macaroni with you?

GIOVANELLI: It is not for the macaroni; it's for the sentiment.

DAISY: The sentiment is yours, not mine. I haven't any: it's all gone.

GIOVANELLI: I will make sure we have the best table, the best wine, and the most delicious food.

DAISY: Let's go there at once!

GIOVANELLI: I hope Mr Winterbourne will do us the honour of joining us for dinner.

WINTERBOURNE: (*Moving towards them stiffly.*) It's only half-past four. Isn't that rather too soon to dine?

DAISY: We can walk through the old streets. I've only ever seen them from a carriage.

GIOVANELLI: Even if we walk, we will still be a little early. Why don't we first take a stroll round the Pincio?

Bells chiming in the distance.

DAISY: (*Pause. Looking at WINTERBOURNE.*) Oh well, if you like. It's so beautiful. The whole of Rome stretched out before us – just as you described it, Mr Winterbourne.

GIOVANELLI: Italy is the most beautiful country in the world – of a beauty so far beyond any other that none other is worth talking about.

DAISY laughs.

I can feel the sunshine. Such heavenly air! I can smell violets in the grass. The old enchantment of Rome takes its own good time, steals over you and possesses you –

DAISY: That's what Mr Winterbourne thinks too.

GIOVANELLI: (*Holding out his hand.*) Viene! Viene!

DAISY moves away with GIOVANELLI.

WINTERBOURNE watches.

After a moment we hear sounds of a carriage drawing up.

MRS WALKER: Frederick! *Frederick!*

MRS WALKER appears looking flustered.

WINTERBOURNE goes to her.

It is really too dreadful. That girl must not do this sort of thing. She must not walk here with you two men. She will have been noticed.

WINTERBOURNE: I think it's a pity to make too much fuss about it.

MRS WALKER: It's a pity to let the girl ruin herself.

WINTERBOURNE: She's very innocent.

MRS WALKER: She's very crazy! Did you ever see anything so blatantly imbecile as the girl's mother? After you had all left me, just now, I could not sit still for thinking of it. It seemed too pitiful, not even to attempt to save her. I ordered the carriage and put on my bonnet, and came here as quickly as possible.

WINTERBOURNE: What do you propose to do with us?

MRS WALKER: Take her for a ride in my carriage. We'll drive around for half an hour, so the world may see she's not running absolutely wild, and then I'll take her safely home.

WINTERBOURNE: I don't think it's a very happy thought, but you can try.

MRS WALKER: You must ask her to come over here to me.

WINTERBOURNE: Very well.

WINTERBOURNE goes towards DAISY and GIOVANELLI.

DAISY turns and goes straight up to MRS WALKER. She puts out her hand.

DAISY: Mrs Walker! What good fortune. Now I can introduce you to Mr Giovanelli. Mr Giovanelli, this is Mrs Walker. Is that your carriage? I don't believe I have ever seen anything so lovely.

MRS WALKER: I'm glad you admire it. Why not come with me and let me take you for a drive?

DAISY: Oh, no, thank you. I shall admire it much more as I see you driving round in it. It would be charming, but I'm quite happy as I am. (*Looks at WINTERBOURNE and GIOVANELLI.*) It's all so enchanting.

MRS WALKER: It may be enchanting, dear child, but it's not the custom here.

DAISY: Well, it ought to be, then! If I didn't walk I should expire.

MRS WALKER: You should walk with your mother, dear.

DAISY: With my mother dear! My mother never walked ten steps in her life. I am more than five years old, you know.

MRS WALKER: You are old enough then, to be more reasonable. You are old enough, dear Miss Miller, to be talked about.

DAISY: Talked about? What do you mean?

MRS WALKER: Come into my carriage and I will tell you.

DAISY: I don't think I want to know what you mean. I don't think I should like it.

MRS WALKER: Should you prefer being thought a very reckless girl?

DAISY: Gracious me! Does Mr Winterbourne think that – to save my reputation – I ought to get into the carriage?

WINTERBOURNE: (*After a pause, gently.*) I think you *should* get into the carriage.

DAISY: (*Laughing.*) I never heard anything so stiff! If this is improper, Mrs Walker, then I'm *all* improper, and you had better give me right up. Good-bye; I hope you'll have a lovely ride! (*She takes MR GIOVANELLI's arm and walks away, holding her head high.*)

MRS WALKER: Frederick, get into the carriage with me.

WINTERBOURNE: I feel bound, Emily, to accompany Miss Miller.

MRS WALKER: If you refuse me this favour, I will never speak to you again.

WINTERBOURNE: You are evidently wound up.

MRS WALKER: Wound up? And who would not be wound up?

WINTERBOURNE: I will go and take my leave of Miss Miller. (*He goes to where DAISY and GIOVANELLI are standing. He takes DAISY on one side.*) Daisy, I must speak to you. We admire you very much, and we hate to see you misjudged. If you could see how little it's the custom here to do what you do, and how badly it looks to fly in the face of the custom, you would be...

DAISY: (*Laughs at his pomposity.*) Look here, Mr Winterbourne, I'm an American, I'm not one of these people. You make too much fuss: that's what's the matter with you! I think you are trying to mystify me: I can tell that by your language. One would never think you were the same person who went with me to that castle.

WINTERBOURNE: If I can't persuade you to come with us in the carriage, then I am afraid I can no longer walk with you.

DAISY shakes his hand without even looking at him. GIOVANELLI, clearly delighted, doffs his cap and bows a little too ostentatiously.

WINTERBOURNE returns to MRS WALKER.

That was not clever of you.

MRS WALKER: In such a case, I don't wish to be clever, I wish to be *true!*

WINTERBOURNE: Well, your truth has only offended her and put her off.

MRS WALKER: All well and good. If she is so determined to compromise herself, the sooner one knows it the better; one can act accordingly.

WINTERBOURNE: I suspect she means no great harm, you know.

MRS WALKER: That's what I thought a month ago.

WINTERBOURNE: What exactly has she been doing?

MRS WALKER: Everything that is not done here.

WINTERBOURNE: What do you mean?

MRS WALKER: Flirting with any man she can pick up; sitting in corners with mysterious Italians; dancing all evening with the same partners; receiving visits at eleven o'clock at night, and now refusing to take my advice.

WINTERBOURNE: But her mother is with her, surely?

MRS WALKER: Her mother melts away when visitors come.

WINTERBOURNE: But her brother sits up till midnight.

MRS WALKER: He must be edified by what he sees. I'm told that at their hotel everyone's talking about her, and that a smile goes round among the servants when a gentleman comes and asks for Miss Miller.

WINTERBOURNE: The servants be hanged! The poor girl's only fault is her lack of a good education.

MRS WALKER: She is naturally indelicate. Take that example this morning. How long had you known her in Vevey?

WINTERBOURNE: A couple of days.

MRS WALKER: Fancy, then, her making it a personal matter that you should have returned to Geneva.

WINTERBOURNE: I suspect, Emily, that you and I have lived too long in Europe.

MRS WALKER: I think you should cease your relations with Miss Daisy Miller at once. I advise you not to flirt with her – in short, to let her alone.

WINTERBOURNE: I'm afraid I can't do that. I like her too much.

MRS WALKER: All the more reason you shouldn't help her to make a scandal.

WINTERBOURNE: There shall be nothing scandalous in my attentions to her.

MRS WALKER: There certainly will be in the way she takes them. But I have had my say. If you wish to rejoin the young lady, that is your affair.

WINTERBOURNE: I would like to walk a little.

MRS WALKER: Very well, I'll leave you here.

She exits.

WINTERBOURNE hesitates before joining DAISY and GIOVANELLI at the balustrade. As he starts towards them he is arrested by what he sees.

The sun has sent out a brilliant shaft of light through a couple of cloud-bars.

GIOVANELLI takes her parasol out of her hands and opens it.

She moves a little nearer to him as he holds it over her.

He lets it rest on her shoulder, so that both their heads are hidden from WINTERBOURNE.

WINTERBOURNE watches them for a few moments, turns and walks off.

The lights fade to blackout.

WINTERBOURNE steps out into a spotlight. He is changing for the evening soirée.

WINTERBOURNE: But what of Daisy? Would a *nice girl* have made such a rendezvous? Charmed – as I was before in Vevey – by her sudden familiarities, but buffeted by her caprices, I have come back to the awkward question of whether in fact she is a nice girl. From the start I had thought of Daisy as a child of nature. Is it possible to regard her as a wholly unspotted flower? She remains an inscrutable combination of audacity and innocence.

Lights up on three days later at MRS WALKER's soirée. Music, conversation and laughter are heard offstage.

MRS MILLER is wandering around on her own. She discovers WINTERBOURNE who has escaped to the ante-room.

MRS MILLER: You see I've come all alone. I'm so frightened; I don't know what to do; it's the first time I've ever been to a party alone – especially in this country. I wanted to bring Randolph or Eugenio, but Daisy pushed me off by myself. I ain't used to going round alone.

MRS WALKER: (*Entering.*) And doesn't your daughter intend to favour us with her society?

MRS MILLER: She's all dressed. She got dressed on purpose before dinner. But she's got a friend of hers with her. That Italian gentleman. They've got going on the piano; it seems as if they couldn't leave off. Mr Giovanelli does sing splendidly. I guess they'll come before very long. I told her there was no use in her getting dressed before dinner if she was going to wait three hours before leaving for the soireé. I didn't see the point of her putting on such a dress as that to just sit round with Mr Giovanelli. I wonder if she came in and I didn't see her. (*She wanders off in search of DAISY.*)

MRS WALKER: This is most horrible! *Elle s'affiche.* Making such a show of herself. It's her revenge for my venturing to remonstrate with her. When she comes I shall not speak to her.

DAISY enters with GIOVANELLI.

She goes straight up to MRS WALKER.

DAISY: I'm afraid you thought I was never coming, so I sent mother off to tell you. I wanted to make Mr Giovanelli practise before he came. He knows the most charming set of songs, and I want you to ask him to sing. This is Mr Giovanelli; you remember I introduced him to you the other day. (*Looking around.*) Is there anyone here I know?

MRS WALKER: (*Coldly, barely acknowledging GIOVANELLI.*) I think everyone knows you! (*She turns her back on them and moves away.*)

DAISY: Aurelio, you go and find the musicians, and give them your music. (*She pushes GIOVANELLI away and then sees WINTERBOURNE.*) Mr Winterbourne! It's a pity these rooms are so small; we can't dance.

WINTERBOURNE: I'm not sorry we cannot dance. I don't dance.

DAISY: Of course you don't dance; you're too stiff! I hope you enjoyed your drive with Mrs Walker.

WINTERBOURNE: I didn't enjoy it. I went for a walk alone.

DAISY: Did you ever hear anything so cool as Mrs
Walker's wanting me to get into her carriage and drop
poor Mr Giovanelli; and under the pretext that it was
proper? It would have been most unkind; Mr Giovanelli
had been talking about that walk for ten days.

*GIOVANELLI's voice can be heard, singing an Italian
song.*

Listen! Hasn't he got a lovely voice? We had the
greatest time at the hotel. I made him go over his songs
again and again. Mrs Walker didn't seem too pleased to
see me, but never mind, she will forgive me now she's
heard Mr Giovanelli sing.

WINTERBOURNE: He would never have proposed to
a young lady of this country to walk about the streets
of Rome with him, let alone invite her to supper in a
tavern.

DAISY: About the streets? Where then would he have
proposed to walk? We took a cab to the *Falcone*. The
Pincio ain't the streets, either, I guess; my Baedeker
guide – you see I've got one – says the Pincio is 'the
safest promenade in Rome', and *I*, thank goodness, am
not a young lady of this country. The young ladies of
this country have a dreadfully pokey time of it, so far as
I can see; I don't see why I should change my habits for
them.

WINTERBOURNE: I'm afraid your habits are those of a
ruthless flirt.

DAISY: Of course they are. I'm a fearful frightful flirt! Did
you ever hear of a nice girl that wasn't? But I suppose
you will tell me now that I am not a nice girl.

WINTERBOURNE: You're a very nice girl, but I wish
you would flirt with me, and me only.

DAISY: Ah! Thank you, thank you very much; you're the last man I should think of flirting with. As I have more than once had the pleasure of informing you, *you are too stiff.*

WINTERBOURNE: (*Annoyed.*) You say that too often.

DAISY: If I could have the sweet hope of making you angry, I would say it again.

WINTERBOURNE: Don't do that; when I'm angry I'm more unbending than ever. But if you won't flirt with me, do cease at least to flirt with your friend at the piano. They don't understand that sort of thing here.

DAISY: I thought they understood nothing else!

WINTERBOURNE: Not in young unmarried women.

DAISY: It seems to me much more proper in young unmarried than in old married ones.

WINTERBOURNE: Well, when in Rome.

DAISY laughs.

Flirting is a purely American custom; it doesn't exist here. So when you show yourself in public with Mr Giovanelli and without your mother –

DAISY: Gracious! Poor mother!

The singing stops. Perfunctory clapping.

WINTERBOURNE: Though *you* may be flirting, Mr Giovanelli is not; he means something else.

DAISY: He isn't preaching, at any rate. And if you really want to know, neither of us is flirting; we are too good friends for that; we're real intimate friends.

GIOVANELLI appears looking flushed with excitement.

WINTERBOURNE: Ah, if you're in love with each other it's another affair altogether!

DAISY: Mr Giovanelli – (*Giving WINTERBOURNE a hard look.*) Mr Giovanelli at least never says such very disagreeable things to me.

She sees GIOVANELLI advancing with a series of bows.

GIOVANELLI: *Carissima signorina.* Did you hear the applause? They liked my singing. Won't you come into the other room and have some tea?

DAISY: It has never occurred to Mr Winterbourne to offer me any tea.

WINTERBOURNE: (*Calling after her.*) I have offered you excellent advice.

DAISY: (*Leaving.*) I prefer weak tea!

A quartet is playing in the background.

MRS WALKER enters.

MRS WALKER: I should never have given her permission to bring that man here. I had to pretend to all my friends that I had no idea who he was, or who brought him. I have to confess though, he sings passably well.

WINTERBOURNE: I have tried to explain to her that her behaviour is unacceptable, but she resolutely refuses to listen to me. I don't know what else I can do.

MRS WALKER: Cease all relations with her at once. When she comes to take her leave, I shall turn my back on her.

WINTERBOURNE: In front of all your guests?

DAISY enters.

DAISY: Mrs Walker, it was ever such a lovely party, and I want to thank you for inviting Mr Giovanelli and me. Didn't Mr Giovanelli sing...

MRS WALKER turns her back on DAISY.

MRS MILLER enters and witnesses the scene.

DAISY looks confused and hurt.

Mrs Walker!

MRS MILLER: (*Flustered.*) Goodnight, Mrs Walker. We've had a perfectly beautiful evening. I hope Daisy took her leave of you in the correct manner. Sometimes she's a bit scatterbrained, but she doesn't mean it. She may come to parties without me but I don't want her to go away without me. Goodnight, Mr Winterbourne. Come along, Daisy.

MRS MILLER, DAISY and GIOVANELLI all leave together.

WINTERBOURNE: That was very cruel.

MRS WALKER: That young lady never enters my drawing-room again!

She exits.

Lights fade.

WINTERBOURNE steps forward into the spotlight and changes out of his evening clothes.

WINTERBOURNE: I am no longer able to meet Daisy in Emily Walker's drawing-room, so I go as often as possible to Mrs Miller's hotel. The ladies are rarely at home, and when they are, Giovanelli is always present. Daisy never seems annoyed or embarrassed by my entrance. I often find the two of them alone, and she chatters away with us both, as freely as with one of us. She appears not to be troubled by jealousy, and shows no displeasure when I interrupt her tête-à-têtes. She is evidently very much interested in Giovanelli, is perpetually telling him to do this and do that, and constantly teases and jokes with him. I begin to feel she has no more surprises for me; the unexpected in her behaviour is the only thing to expect. In an odd way I rather like not having to make out what she is up to.

Lights up on MRS COSTELLO's apartment in Rome a few weeks later.

Noises of carnival, and street band.

MRS COSTELLO closes the window.

MRS COSTELLO: This Carnival goes on too long. I say the same thing every year. The tooting and piping and fiddling haven't stopped for a week, and my poor old head has been racked with pain. You're very preoccupied, Frederick; you've been like this for the past six weeks; you're always thinking of something.

WINTERBOURNE: And what is it you accuse me of thinking of?

MRS COSTELLO: Of that young, Miss Baker's, Miss Chandler's – what's her name? – Miss Miller's intrigue with that barber's block.

WINTERBOURNE: Do you call it an intrigue, aunt, an affair that goes on with such publicity?

MRS COSTELLO: That's their folly, it's not their merit.

WINTERBOURNE: No, I don't believe there's anything to be called an intrigue.

MRS COSTELLO: I've heard a dozen people speak of it, saying she is quite carried away by him.

WINTERBOURNE: They certainly seem very intimate.

MRS COSTELLO: He's very handsome, I grant you
that. One easily sees how it is. She thinks he's the most
elegant gentleman in the world. She has never seen
anyone like him; he's even better than the courier.

WINTERBOURNE: I don't believe she thinks of marrying
him.

MRS COSTELLO: You may be sure she thinks of nothing.
She romps on from day to day, from hour to hour, as
they did in the Golden Age. I can imagine nothing
more vulgar. She will be telling you any moment she is
engaged.

WINTERBOURNE: I think that is more than Giovanelli
expects.

MRS COSTELLO: Who is Giovanelli?

WINTERBOURNE: The little Italian. Obviously he is
immensely charmed with Miss Miller, but I really doubt
if he dreams of marrying her. That would appear to him
far beyond the realms of possibility.

MRS COSTELLO: I disagree. I think he can't believe
his luck at being taken up by her. To him anything is
possible!

WINTERBOURNE: But he has nothing except his
handsome face to offer, and there's a substantial, a
possibly explosive Mr Miller in that mysterious land of
dollars and six-shooters.

MRS COSTELLO: Any man who can send his family to
Europe, to be accompanied only by an over-familiar
courier, deserves all he gets.

WINTERBOURNE: Giovanelli's very conscious that
he hasn't a title to offer. If only he were a count or a
marchese! What on earth can he make of the way she has
taken him up?

MRS COSTELLO: He doesn't need a title. He accounts for it by his handsome face and thinks Miss Miller a young lady *qui se passe ses fantasies!* Mark my words, it was probably the courier who introduced them, and if he succeeds in marrying the young lady, the courier will come in for a magnificent commission.

MRS COSTELLO exits.

WINTERBOURNE steps into a spotlight.

WINTERBOURNE: The following day I saw Daisy at the Palace of the Caesars. She was moving with ease over the mounds of the ruin watched by a glowing Giovanelli. It seemed to me at that moment that Rome had never been so lovely. The spring air was filled with perfume, and the rugged surface of the Palatine was newly green. The freshness of the year mingled wonderfully with the antiquity of the place. It seemed to me also that Daisy had never looked so utterly charming. I wanted to go and speak to her, but knew that at the moment she only wanted to be with Giovanelli. An open carriage was waiting for them, and they drove away for all the world to see. I felt overcome by pity for her. It was painful to see so much that was lovely and undefended and natural sink so low in the eyes of her fellow countrymen...

Lights up on MRS MILLER's hotel.

Sounds of the carnival going on outside in the street.

MRS MILLER turns from the balcony where she has been watching the carnival.

MRS MILLER: I'm so sorry, Mr Winterbourne, but Daisy's not here. I keep telling her that you have called many times. She's gone to the Carnival with Mr Giovanelli. She's always going round with Mr Giovanelli. It seems as if they couldn't live without each other! Well, he's a real gentleman anyhow. I guess I have a joke with Daisy – that she *must* be engaged.

WINTERBOURNE: And how does your daughter *take* the joke?

MRS MILLER: Oh, she says she ain't. But she might as well be! She goes on as if she was. But I've made Mr Giovanelli promise to tell me, if Daisy don't. I should want to write to Mr Miller about it – wouldn't you?

WINTERBOURNE: Certainly I would. Mrs Miller, I came here today to talk to you about Daisy. Her behaviour is arousing a great deal of criticism. Daisy hasn't even noticed that she's been ostracised. I am only telling you this for her own good. I don't want to see Daisy get hurt.

MRS MILLER: It's no good coming to me with these tales. Daisy does what she likes. Oh, dear, I wish my husband were here. (*She starts to cry.*) I really want to go home, Mr Winterbourne.

She runs out of the room.

DAISY enters with GIOVANELLI. They are laughing and carrying carnival masks.

GIOVANELLI has a tin trumpet, which he is blowing.

DAISY holds her mask up and peers at WINTERBOURNE.

DAISY: You look lonesome, Mr Winterbourne.

WINTERBOURNE: Lonesome?

DAISY: You are always going round by yourself.

WINTERBOURNE: I am not so fortunate as your companion.

DAISY: We've been up and down the Corso in an open carriage. We could see everything from there. Mr

Giovanelli says the illumination is better than usual, and the music especially lively. (*She goes to the window and leans out.*) Listen to the music – listen to it, Aurelio!

WINTERBOURNE: (*Taking DAISY's arm.*) Perhaps, Miss Miller, you should spend more time with your mother, and Randolph.

DAISY: I know why you say that. You think I go round too much with *him.*

WINTERBOURNE: Everyone thinks so – if you care to know.

DAISY: Of course I care to know! But I don't believe a word of it. They are only pretending to be shocked. They don't really care a straw what I do. Besides, I don't go round so much.

WINTERBOURNE: I think you will discover they do care, and they will show it – disagreeably.

DAISY: How – disagreeably?

WINTERBOURNE: Haven't you noticed anything?

DAISY: I've noticed *you.* But I noticed you stiff as an umbrella the first time I saw you.

WINTERBOURNE: You will find I am not so unyielding and disagreeable as several others.

DAISY: How shall I find it?

WINTERBOURNE: By going to see the others.

DAISY: What will they do to me?

WINTERBOURNE: They will give you the cold shoulder. Do you know what that means?

DAISY: Do you mean as Mrs Walker did at her soirée?

WINTERBOURNE: Exactly.

DAISY: I wouldn't think you'd let people be so unkind!

WINTERBOURNE: How can I help it?

DAISY: I should think you'd want to say something.

WINTERBOURNE: I do want to say something. I want to say that your mother tells me she believes you are engaged to Mr Giovanelli.

DAISY: Well, I guess she does.

WINTERBOURNE: And does Randolph believe it?

DAISY: I guess Randolph doesn't believe anything.

WINTERBOURNE laughs.

But since you have mentioned it, I *am* engaged.

She looks at GIOVANELLI.

WINTERBOURNE stops laughing and looks at her.

You don't believe it!

WINTERBOURNE: (*Pause.*) Yes, I believe it.

DAISY: Oh no, you don't! But *if* you possibly do – well, I ain't!

She leaves with GIOVANELLI without a backward glance.

Lights fade on MRS MILLER's hotel.

WINTERBOURNE steps forward in his spotlight.

WINTERBOURNE: Daisy has now been completely ostracised by the American community in Rome. They want to make it clear to their European friends, that although she is a very pretty American girl, her behaviour is far from pretty; that in fact it is quite monstrous; and that they wish fully to be disassociated from her and her behaviour. I can't make out if Daisy is aware of this, or whether she is too hopelessly childish and shallow to even notice. Whatever it is, I miss her, and now it is too late, too late. She has been carried away by Giovanelli. A week later, I had been out to dinner with some friends at their beautiful villa on the Caelian Hill. It was a perfect evening, so I dismissed the cab and decided to go home on foot. I walked under the Arch of Constantine, and passed the vaguely lighted monuments of the Forum on my way to the Colosseum. I have never been able to resist the chance to see the Colosseum by moonlight, and that night the moon, though only half full, was brilliant. The Colosseum had never seemed more impressive. I was aware as I walked to one of the empty arches, that there was an open carriage parked outside. And then I saw Daisy.

The Colosseum.

Moonlight.

WINTERBOURNE enters and stands in the shadows.

DAISY: There's a man over there, staring at us. He's like one of the old lions or tigers looking at the Christian martyrs you've been telling me about.

GIOVANELLI: Let us hope he's not very hungry. He'll have to take me first, and you for dessert!

DAISY laughs.

WINTERBOURNE steps out of the shadows as though to go towards them, and then changes his mind.

DAISY looks up suddenly.

DAISY: Why, it's Mr Winterbourne! He saw me – and he cut me! (*Calling.*) Mr Winterbourne!

WINTERBOURNE turns round again and goes up to DAISY.

You saw me, didn't you, and turned away. Why, Mr Winterbourne?

WINTERBOURNE: (*Speaking almost brutally.*) How long have you been fooling round here?

DAISY: Well, I guess all the evening – we've seen the sun setting and the moon rising. I never saw anything so pretty.

WINTERBOURNE: I am afraid that you will not think Roman fever very pretty. This is the way people catch it. (*To GIOVANELLI.*) I wonder that you, a native Roman, should countenance such extraordinary rashness.

GIOVANELLI: For myself, I am not afraid.

WINTERBOURNE: Neither am I – for you! I am speaking for this young lady.

GIOVANELLI: I told the Signorina it was a grave indiscretion; but when was the Signorina ever prudent?

DAISY: I never was sick, and I don't mean to be! I don't look like much, but I'm healthy. I just *had* to see the Colosseum by moonlight; I shouldn't have wanted to go home without that; and we have had the most beautiful time, haven't we, Aurelio?

GIOVANELLI: Perfetto, Signorina.

DAISY: Eugenio can always give me some pills. He has some splendid pills.

WINTERBOURNE: I should advise you to drive home as fast as possible and take one!

GIOVANELLI: What you say is very wise, I will go and make sure the carriage is ready. (*He leaves.*)

DAISY: (*Rather embarrassed.*) Well, I *have* seen the Colosseum by moonlight! That's one good thing.

WINTERBOURNE remains silent.

Why aren't you speaking to me? (*Pause.*) *Did* you believe I was engaged the other day?

WINTERBOURNE: It doesn't matter what I believed the other day.

DAISY: Well, what do you believe now?

WINTERBOURNE: I believe that it makes very little difference whether you are engaged or not!

DAISY is about to reply but GIOVANELLI rushes in.

GIOVANELLI: Quick, quick, if we get in by midnight we are quite safe.

He takes her arm.

WINTERBOURNE calls after them.

WINTERBOURNE: Don't forget Eugenio's pills!

DAISY: (*Stopping in her tracks.*) I don't care whether I have Roman fever or not!

WINTERBOURNE watches her go.

WINTERBOURNE: I mentioned to no one that I encountered Daisy and Giovanelli at the Colosseum, but no doubt there would have been an exchange of jokes between the porter and the cab-driver when she arrived back at the hotel, and the news of her scandalous adventure soon reached the ears of the American circle. I became aware that it was not a matter of serious regret to me that Daisy was being gossiped about by her compatriots in Rome, and by servants and cab-drivers. Then I heard that Daisy was dangerously ill with malaria; despite her defiant remark about not caring if she got Roman fever, the poor girl had, indeed, fallen victim to it.

Lights up on MRS MILLER's hotel room.

MRS MILLER: Daisy spoke of you the other day quite pleasantly. Half the time she doesn't know what she's saying, but on that occasion I think she did.

WINTERBOURNE: What did she say?

MRS MILLER: She gave me a message; she told me to tell you that she never was engaged to that handsome Italian. I am sure I am very glad; Mr Giovanelli hasn't been near us since she was taken ill. I thought he was so much of a gentleman; but I don't call that very polite!

WINTERBOURNE: He's probably ashamed for having taken her out at night and exposed her to such danger.

MRS MILLER: I should think so too. I am very angry, but I suppose he knows I'm a lady. I would scorn to scold him. Anyway she says she's not engaged. I don't know why she wanted you to know; but she said to me three times – 'Mind you tell Mr Winterbourne.'

WINTERBOURNE: Did she say anything else?

MRS MILLER: Yes she did. (*She reaches into her pocket and takes out a piece of paper.*) She made me write it down. She said it was a surprise for when you went to Keats's House together, and she was sorry she couldn't keep her promise. (*She hands the paper to WINTERBOURNE.*)

WINTERBOURNE: (*Reads.*)
When old age shall this generation waste,
Thou shalt remain, in midst of other woe
Than ours, a friend to man, to whom thou say'st,
Beauty is truth, truth beauty – that is all
Ye know on earth, and all ye need to know.

(*Visibly moved.*) Did she recite this to you?

MRS MILLER: Yes. I couldn't quite make out what she was saying as she kept rambling, but she said she had learnt the whole poem, and you would understand. And then she told me to ask if you remembered the time you went to the castle, in Switzerland. But I said I wouldn't give any such messages as that. Only, if she's not engaged, I'm sure glad to know it.

A bell rings off stage.

I must go to her. Please excuse me, Mr Winterbourne.

She exits.

A single bell tolls throughout the next scene.

Some daisies have been placed on the grave and are now wilting.

WINTERBOURNE: I went back often to ask after Daisy, but was never allowed to see her. I was impressed by Mrs Miller's dignity and good sense. Though obviously deeply shocked and worried by her daughter's condition, she proved to be a perfectly composed and judicious nurse; not the worthless person that I and others had so unthinkingly taken her to be. She was not, after all, such a monstrous goose. Daisy died a few days later. They found a small plot for the girl from Schenectady in the little Protestant Cemetery, in an angle of the wall of imperial Rome, beneath the cypresses, not far from where Keats and Shelley are laid to rest. (*Reading the epitaph on her tombstone.*)

'If thou art young and lovely, build not thereon, for she who lieth beneath thy feet in death was the loveliest flower ever cropt in its bloom.' Annie P Miller known and loved as Daisy. 1860 – 1879.

WINTERBOURNE moves away into the shadows.

Should I blame myself for her death? Could I have saved her? Did I stand back too far, always the detached observer? These questions still trouble me, and I can't get Daisy out of my mind

GIOVANELLI enters carrying a fresh bunch of daisies. He kneels down and removes the dead flowers and replaces them with the fresh ones.

GIOVANELLI: You were the most beautiful young lady I ever saw. The most amiable and – the most innocent.

WINTERBOURNE emerges from the shadows.

WINTERBOURNE: And the most innocent?

GIOVANELLI: The most innocent!

WINTERBOURNE: Why the devil did you take her to that fatal place?

GIOVANELLI: As you know, for myself I had no fear; and she wanted to go.

WINTERBOURNE: That was no reason.

GIOVANELLI: If she had lived I should have got nothing. She would never have married me, I am sure.

WINTERBOURNE: She would never have married you?

GIOVANELLI: For a moment I hoped so. But no, I am sure.

GIOVANELLI leaves.WINTERBOURNE stays looking at the grave.

Fade to a spotlight on WINTERBOURNE. He hears DAISY's voice.

DAISY: Give me my Romeo; and, when he shall die,
Take him and cut him out in little stars,
And he will make the face of heaven so fine
That all the world will be in love with night
And pay no worship to the garish sun.

As the lights fade on WINTERBOURNE we gradually become aware of another image.

It is DAISY as we first saw her – but it is a ghostly image in the moonlight.

Stars start to twinkle in the sky and then a slow fade to black.

The End.